F.
BOY'S
GUIDE

A BOY'S GUIDE

Written by

Ipshita Bose

First published in 2011 by

Media Eight Publishing

India Private Limited

302-A, ABW Tower, M G Road
Gurgaon 122001, India
Tel: 0124 4040017

ISBN: 978-81-7314-222-2

Printed in India by
Gopsons Papers Ltd.

Contents

Introduction...9

Game On & Be a Sport!
Sports and Gaming...............................11
    Gaming...12
    Sports...27

Keeping Busy!
Hobbies & Activities...........................53
    Paintball...55
    Say Cheese!...59
    Boy Scouts...63
    Collectorama!..66
    Hiking...71
    Rappelling and Rock Climbing.................74

Vroom!
Mean Machines..**77**

    Cars...79

    Bikes..91

Having Fun!
Entertainment...**99**

    Music, the Soul Food...................................101

    For Bookworms...112

    Movie Buffs...123

Looking Fit & Muscling Up!
Health and Fitness...**137**

    Health..138

    Fitness..150

Introduction

For all the young teens out there (and this means guys only!), this is the book you have been waiting for. This is one book that every teen boy must have alongside all his other favourite authors on the bookshelf. It definitely deserves a place among your most cherished books. If you don't believe us, then go ahead and give it a read!

A Boy's Guide has it all: sports, gaming, adrenaline-rising high speed cars and bikes, adventurous and thrilling activities, a must-watch list of movies, a few books that you absolutely must read, a great collection of music for all times and so much more. From the legendary and classic oldies to the contemporary and modern, this book has it all. There are numerous handy tips and information tidbits on a range of topics that you will definitely find interesting. If something doesn't quite get your interest, just flip a few pages and find what you are looking for! So you see, this book does have it all.

This book is a handy reference to almost everything a guy wants to know. Hard-hitting sports, cool music, engaging books, stimulating hobbies—you name it and we've got it! If you are a die-hard movie

addict and proud to admit it, then we have a list of amazing movies which you should have on your must-watch list. If you are an avid book reader and a self proclaimed bookworm, then again we bring you a plethora of books which should be sitting proudly on your bookshelf. Call yourself something of an expert on the subject of cars and bikes; well we have a few more amazing vehicles you should have a look at.

Then again, if you are a bit of a bookworm, but would like to know more about some lean mean machines, then the section on cars and bikes is going to blow you away with a collection of some of the most talked about and slick four wheel drives and some pretty amazing bikes. For all the guys who would rather stay away from books, we have a great compilation of books which are not only a good read but they also contain some incredible life lessons. So go ahead and try reading a few of the books listed here and you are sure to get hooked.

It is a great guide for young boys entering their teens, leaving their toy trucks and cars behind and stepping into the world of gaming and serious sports. The following pages contain everything, ranging from exhilarating hobbies, rocking entertainment to some serious information on eating healthy and keeping fit. So go ahead and start reading and discover a wealth of information and fun! Enjoy!

Game On
&
Be a Sport!

Sports and Gaming

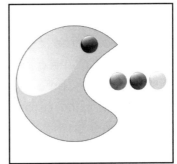

Gaming

Do you like going head-to-head with some of the toughest teams of football in FIFA, breaking the speed limit and crashing into corners in Grand Theft Auto, sneaking-up on the enemy in Counter Strike, coming up with impressive strategies in Age of Empires, role playing in World of Warcraft or just playing house with Sims? If you have heard these names before, then you know that we are talking about one of the world's favourite pastimes, gaming!

All these games are known as electronic games and are played on the computer, TV, handheld consoles and so on. Did you know that the first electronic game was made using an oscilloscope, some push buttons and an analogue computer? It resulted in the first interactive game called Tennis for Two. However, gaming has come a long way since then and thanks to the advancement in technology, gaming has undergone quite a revolution. Now, apart from the video games on the computer and the arcade games, we also have gaming on handheld consoles like the

Sony PlayStation, the Xbox, iPads, mobile phones and not to forget - the Nintendo Wii. These devices are perfect when you have a day planned with lots of buttered popcorn, cola, nachos, a group of friends and want to play a multiplayer game. The dynamic graphics, powerful sound system, complex game strategies and lifelike simulations - all make gaming a great source of entertainment enjoyed by the young and the old. So don't be too surprised if you walk in on your grandfather playing on your PlayStation!

Gaming History

Did you know that video games were first devised by students in universities in the United States and were developed as a hobby? The first widely available and most prominent game was called 'Spacewar!' and then came 'Chase', which could be seen on TV. After this, the 'light gun' was created. It was a gun-shaped pointing device used in computer games and arcade consoles. This gave rise to many more video games.

The 1970s saw the Golden Age of arcade games. 'Galaxy Game' was the first coin operated game. Then came many such games like 'Pong', 'Space Invaders', 'Asteroids' and the still favourite, 'Pac-Man'! During this golden age, you would find kids

saving up their pocket money to go play at these gaming arcades, which could be found in restaurants, shopping malls, convenience stores and so on.

During the 1980s, adventure games such as 'Zork' and 'King's Quest' became very popular. Even games based on martial arts, like 'Karate Champ' and 'Street Fighter', were developed. Then came the craze of platform games with the invention of 'Space Panic' - the first ever platform game, 'Donkey Kong', an arcade game created by Nintendo's and the very popular and loved by all 'Mario Bros.', which was a single player game and also introduced collaborative play. Then came 'Prince of Persia' in 1989, which was later an inspiration for the popular game 'Prince of Persia' developed in 2010. (This game proved to be an inspiration for the 2010 box office grossing movie - Prince of Persia: The Sands of Time.)

The 1990s brought in new ideas with the introduction of Game Boy and huge online multiplayer games. It was the 90s which brought us, 'Sonic Hedgehog', and 'Warcraft: Orcs and Humans'. It also saw the founding of real-time strategy games like the much-loved Microsoft's 'Age of Empires' and Blizzard's 'Warcraft'.

The 2000s came with the Xbox, the Xbox 360, the Sony PlayStations, the Nintendo Game Cube and Wii. These video game consoles revolutionised gaming and introduced some of the world's favourite games like the 'Grand Theft Auto' series, 'Call of Duty: Black Ops', 'Need for Speed', 'Midtown Madness', the 'Halo' series and much more. We were introduced to the very fascinating world of 'Sims', the challenging strategies of 'World of Warcraft' and the lifelike characters of the 'Final Fantasy' series.

Gamers

A gamer is someone who spends much of his time learning about and playing different video games. This does not mean that a gamer eats, sleeps and talks only games! If you like playing video games a lot and sometimes wish that the time you have to spend studying algebra could be spent playing your favourite games, then even you are a gamer! Did you know that just like there are different types of games, there are different types of gamers?

Casual Gamers

For casual gamers, gaming is a source of entertainment, enjoyment and a way to pass the time. Casual gamers usually play online, consoles and computer-based games, which have simple rules and require no long-term commitment or special skills to play. Many of these gamers indulge in gaming to connect with

friends and to socialise. A casual gamer can also be a fitness gamer who plays motion-based games as it provides a fun way to stay fit!

Hardcore Gamers

In the 1970s, hardcore gamers usually played the now classic 'Pac-Man', 'Donkey Kong', 'Tetris', 'Snake' and so on. But hardcore gaming today is a whole new ball game. Just because you can play 'Counter Strike' and 'Call of Duty', you do not become a hardcore gamer. To be one, you need to have a deep passion for the art of gaming and be a pro at playing both kinds of games like 'New Super Mario Bros.' and 'Halo 3'. Hardcore gamers also take part in structured competitions, tournaments and leagues.

Pro Gamers

A pro gamer is someone who is in the business of gaming because of his passion and the money that comes with it! Pro gamers do not consider gaming as a hobby or a pastime, but as a serious career. They are hardcore gamers who have turned what they love doing, into their profession. It is one of the best examples of doing what you love for a living. Pro gamers are also supported by major companies, especially in Asia, South Korea and Japan where gaming is huge.

Newbie

Newbie or a 'noob' is someone who is new to the world of gaming or to one game in particular. The best example of a newbie would be your dad. This is when he sits down beside you while you are furiously thumbing away on your PSP, takes the console from you, rolls up his sleeve and says, "Son, you are now about to see some magic. Your ol' dad used to be the number one player back in his time and the champion of 'Pong' (an arcade game)". This is when you roll your eyes and realise that your dad is a newbie and you go on to explain to him that 'Pong' no longer exists and that the gaming world has now advanced!

Import Gamers

Import gamers are those guys who buy international games which are not available in their country and have to be imported. For example, Anime- and Manga-based games are not easily found outside Japan. Many gamers also do this to improve their language skills, like the Japanese, who import games dubbed in English from other countries. Some die-hard fans can't wait for a particular edition to release in their country and so buy that game from a country where it has already released.

Retro Gamers

Don't be fooled by the name because a retro gamer does not mean an old stick-in-the-mud. A retro gamer, also known as a classic gamer or old school gamer, plays and collects old classics from the world of gaming such as 'Pac-Man', 'Konami', 'Street Fighter', 'Mario', 'Galga' and so on. These games are played either on the original hardware or the modern hardware using ports and compilations.

Girl Gamers

Yes, it's true! Girls like playing video games too. In fact, there are many girls who play way better than any guy. It has been found in a survey that 25 percent of console players and 39 percent of PC players comprise of the female population. Maybe that girl you have a crush on is an awesome gamer and this would surely give you a good chance to start a friendship based on gaming!

Avatars

Don't confuse this with James Cameron's movie 'Avatar' because an avatar in the gaming world has nothing to do with the blue-faced 'Na'vi' or planet Pandora. A gaming avatar is a pseudonym, screen name, alias and so on created by a gamer in a gaming community. A gamer creates an avatar in multiplayer gaming situations or gaming conventions. Avatar gamers can form clans and each gamer of that clan has a clan tag. So what's your avatar or clan tag?

Some Popular Games

1. Call of Duty: Black Ops

"A lie is a lie.
Just because they write it down and call it history
doesn't make it the truth. We live in a world where
seeing is not believing. We live in a world where
everything we know is wrong."

- Frank Woods in the world premier trailer

The seventh instalment to the Call of Duty series, Call of Duty: Black Ops has taken the gaming world by storm. Developed by Treyarch and published by Activision, this game was released worldwide on November 9, 2010. Black Ops is a first

person shooter game where the player takes on the role of special forces operative Alex Mason, a soldier in the elite Black Ops forces and fights in secret wars against the backdrop of the Cold War. With Hind helicopters, grenades, crossbows, ballistic knives and a range of other weapons, Black Ops promises to deliver an exhilarating and explosive adventure.

2. Counter Strike

 Considered as one of the world's best online action game series, Counter Strike also known as Half Life is again a strategic, first person shooter game developed by Valve Corporation. The Counter Strike series include Counter-Strike: Condition Zero, Counter-Strike: Source, Counter-Strike: Anthology and Counter-Strike on Xbox. The player can choose from eight different characters either on the terrorist team or the counter-terrorist squad. The objective is to complete the mission, which includes diffusing bombs, rescuing hostages and obliterating the enemy.

The popularity of Counter Strike has resulted in it being played in LAN tournaments like the ESWC (Electronic Sports World Cup), WCG (World Cyber Games) and the WEG (World e-Sports games).

3. Grand Theft Auto

Grand Theft Auto, more popularly known as GTA, is a series created by Dave Jones and later by Dan Houser and Sam Houser and published by Rockstar Games. Featuring voice-overs from well known celebrities like Ray Liotta, Burt Reynolds, Samuel L. Jackson and so on, Grand Theft Auto is all about a guy who tries to rise in the ranks of the criminal world. The player assumes the role of a small time criminal in a big city and has to complete missions given by the kingpins of the lawless world. GTA has it all, bikes, street races, helicopter pursuits and what not!

4. World of Warcraft

Also known as WoW, World of Warcraft is a huge online multiplayer role playing game developed by Blizzard Entertainment. The player takes on the role of an avatar from the rival clans of either Alliance or Horde, who goes on quests, fights monsters and interacts with other players. As the character keeps evolving, he starts acquiring more talents and

skills. While playing WoW, you can immerse yourself in the land of Azeroth, a world of sword fights and sorcery, which has a variety of races ruled by kings, queens, chieftains, archdruids and many more. This epic fantasy game has magic, mystery and huge dollops of adventure. You can either play it solo or share the virtual experience with thousands of other players.

5. Need for Speed

 Published by EA Games, Need for Speed or NFS is the ultimate game series in the genre of car racing. The goal of the game is obviously to win the race, but NFS offers much more than just car racing from one point to another. In this game series, you can choose your race track, the car you want to drive and the transmission of the car. Piled high with street racing, police chases, drifting, dragging and manoeuvring in jam-packed traffic, this series is sure to thrill and excite. Anyone who gets behind these hot wheels not only gets the thrill of racing, but also an extensive range of muscle cars, rare and exotic cars, tuner cars and special vehicles. NFS will keep you on the edge of your seat!

6. The Sims

A favourite with casual gamers, The Sims was developed by Maxis and published By EA (Electronic Art). Recorded to be the best selling PC game, The Sims is a lifelike simulation game which deals with the daily workings of a suburban household. The game as such does not have a particular objective; the various characters are made to interact with nearby objects and with each other. Every Sims family starts out with §16,000 and the player has to help them go about their daily lives. The Sims are pretty much like normal human beings who pay their bills, go on jobs, give birth, engage in skill development activities and so on, except that the player can control the Sims' actions and responses. So go ahead and start playing The Sims!

7. Gran Turismo

Another popular racing series, Gran Turismo has been developed for the Sony PlayStations by Polyphony Digital and produced by Kazunori Yamauchi. This series

has some amazing graphics, the ability to tune your performance, reallife driving techniques, iconographic simulation and much more. The players start out with 10,000 credits that they use to buy a car and then tune it to its best performance. By winning races, the player can access more cars and different race courses. You can take part in different competitions and win prize money and upgrade the level of your licenses, so that you can participate in various races. So hop on and start the ignition!

8. Mario

Developed by Shigeru Miyamoto, this little man in blue overalls and red cap is recognised by everyone in the gaming world and is now a legend! Did you know he was originally meant to be 'Mr. Video', but was finally named after Miyamoto's landlord, Mario Segale. Mario made his debut as 'Jumpman' in Donkey Kong and never looked back! He was then seen in many Mario games like, Super Mario Bros., Super Mario Land, Super Mario World, Super Mario 64 and not to forget the very famous Mario Bros. Nintendo recently came out with New Super Mario Bros. Wii in 2009 and as can be expected of the Mario Bros., this game too has become popular all over the gaming world.

9. Pac-Man

This game is a classic in the world of gaming and almost synonymous with the term 'video games'. Developed by Namco, it took over the first place in popularity from the very start. The best arcade game ever, Pac-Man has wooed gamers from the young to the old, boys and girls alike. In this game, the player takes control of Pac-Man and manoeuvres through the maze by eating the pellets and avoiding the four enemies - Blinky, Pinky, Inky and Clyde. Pac-Man has had an impact not only on the gaming world but also on the world in general. There is a wide variety of Pac-Man merchandise which has been doing the rounds, and is also a business term for mergers and acquisitions!

A list of some other popular games:

FIFA

Dragon Age II

Tron: Evolution

Shogun II: Total War

Fallout: New Vegas

Two Worlds II

Starcraft II: Wings of Liberty

Dragon Age: Origins

Halo 3

Star Wars: Battlefront

Final Fantasy VII

Final Fantasy XI

Tomb Raider

Mortal Kombat

Sports

Football

Known as one of the world's most popular sports, football fever is something everyone wants to catch! During the football world cup, the whole world is glued to their television sets and it has been recorded that the most number of toilet flushes happen during the football world cup advertisement breaks!

Football, also known as Association Football or Soccer as it is known in the USA, is one of the world's oldest sports. It was played as early as the times of the ancient Greeks and Romans. The Greek version of modern day football was known as '*Episkyros*' and the Romans later adapted it into a similar kind of sport called '*Harpastum*'. In China, the sport was known as '*Cuju*' literally translated as 'kick ball'. It was played by kicking a leather ball through a hole in a silk cloth, which was tied to bamboo canes (think ancient goalposts!). *Cuju* was later adapted by the Japanese into a sport called '*Kemari*'. It is still played

in Japan during festivals. So we now know that your favourite sport of football is being played since the 8th century B.C.

Association Football is the football which is commonly known by everyone. Otherwise football could also mean Rugby, Canadian Football, Gaelic Football and so on. The basic know-how about football is that it is played according to a set of rules, using a single round ball and two teams containing 11 to 18 players each. A team scores against the rival team by kicking the ball into the opposing team's in-goal area. If they manage to do that, they score a goal or a point and the crowds scream "GOAL!" The opposing team defends itself by placing a goalkeeper between the two goal posts to prevent the ball from going in. The team which has the highest number of goals wins the game.

The rules of the sport, also known as the Laws of the Game, state that the players, other than the goal keepers, cannot touch the ball with their hands while playing, except during a throw in. The players advance towards the opposing team's goal by propelling, dribbling or passing the ball to another team mate. The players play on different positions. These positions are strikers or forwards, who try to score a goal; defenders, who prevent their opponents from scoring; and midfielders, who try to throw off the opposition and keep control of the ball so that they can pass it to the forwards, who try to score a goal. Each team is led by a captain. There are also central defenders, and left and right midfielders. The players can be positioned in any way keeping their game strategies in mind. There could be three defenders, four midfielders and three forwards, or four defenders, four midfielders and two forwards. The number of players in each position determines the style of the team's play. More defenders and lesser number of forwards indicates a defensive strategy whereas more forwards and fewer defenders points to a more aggressive and offensive style of play.

Cricket

 The world's second most favourite sport and we are not talking about the insect! This bat and ball sport has won hearts all over the world. The sport of cricket is so popular that it has been named as the de facto national game of many countries.

Cricket, also known as 'The Gentleman's Game', is being played since a long time. It has a history spanning from the 16th century to the present day. The

29

game originated in England, probably invented by the Saxons or Normans during the medieval times. It is generally believed that in the beginning cricket was a children's game just as it is now also loved by kids all over the world, before it was taken up by the grown ups. The name 'Cricket' does not come from the cricket insect. In fact, it has its origins in the old English language where '*cricc*' means a staff or crutch. It was probably called '*Crekett*' back in the days by the Middle Dutch for whom the word '*krick*' means stick.

Cricket is a 'bat and ball' team sport played between two teams of eleven players each. It is played on an oval grass field with a narrow white strip of 22 yards called the cricket pitch. At both the ends of the pitch are three wooden stumps called wickets. The two teams toss to decide which team will bat first and which one will bowl. The team which opts to bat will send two of their batters on the field, who will take their place at the opposite ends of the pitch just before the wickets. The other team will have all its members present on the field, with one as a bowler and the other team members as fielders. The team which chooses to bat will try to score as many runs as possible. This happens when the batsman strikes the ball with the bat and runs to the other end and exchanges places with his partner. This will be counted as scoring a run. The opposing team will try to stop the runs or dismiss the batsmen by retrieving the ball as quickly as possible or by knocking down the wickets before the batsmen reach the crease. The batter will then be run out and would have to quit the field. Then another batsman will replace him. The teams switch between batting and fielding and the batting team takes up bowling and the bowling team sends two batsmen to the field. This takes place at the end of an inning. An inning is the time period till when the batting team bats and till 10 of the 11 batsmen in the team are out.

There are many other adaptations of the game, for example Twenty20, which has 20 overs (over is a set of six consecutive balls bowled in succession) for both the teams and the longest cricket match, which is played over five days, known as Test Cricket. Another type of cricket match played is the ODI or the One Day International. These matches have a different style of play and a different set of rules. The rules of the Twenty20 have Laws of Cricket maintained by the ICC (International Cricket Council), whereas the MCC (Marylebone Cricket Club) maintains the additional Standard Playing Conditions for Test matches and One Day Internationals.

The sporting equipment with which cricket is played includes a cricket ball, a bat, wooden stumps, bails and protective gear. The cricket ball is made of hard cork and covered in leather. It is a bit like a baseball

but the leather covering is thicker. The ball is red in colour with a white stitching running around it. The blade of the cricket bat is made of willow wood. It is flat on one side and gently raised on the other. The bat length is always 38 inches. The three wooden stumps, which make up the wickets, are an inch in diameter and 32 inches in height. Bails are the two wooden pieces which sit in the grooves on top of the three stumps. Protective gear is always necessary when playing cricket. The batsmen are required to wear pads, helmets and gloves because when you are a batsman and a hard leather cork ball is hurtling towards you at fast speed, you need to make sure that you don't end up in the hospital in case you miss!

Hockey

One of the best played ball and stick sport, hockey has a history dating back to the pre-historic times! This sport brings with it fierce and raw passion and one of the best examples of true sportsmanship.

The first known evidence of hockey probably comes from an old Egyptian tomb belonging to Prince Kheti of 2000 B.C. One wall of the tomb is decorated by a drawing of two men holding curved sticks, locked over a ball. A familiar scene that can be seen in any 21st century poster for hockey! However, hockey was being played by other ancient civilisations as well. The Greeks were playing it in 514 B.C., the Araucano Indians of Argentina were playing an ancient game called '*Cheuca*'. It is said that the Persians introduced the sport to the world, or perhaps the Ethiopians or the Arabs and so on. Whether it was hockey or not, all these older civilisations were playing some form of a 'ball and stick' sport. Hockey, is therefore, one of the world's oldest known sports, predating even the 'Ancient Games of Olympia'. The sport has been known by many names, but the closest to the term 'hockey' is probably '*Hockie*' found in a 16th century Irish document. However, there is reason to believe that the term has French origins and was coined from the French *hocquet*, which means 'shepherd's crook'.

Hockey is of two types - Field Hockey and Ice Hockey. The game play is similar, however the rules differ and Ice Hockey is played on ice. The modern game of hockey probably developed in the British Isles in the 19th century and was played by schoolchildren. The sport, as we know it today, was actually invented by cricket players! The Teddington Cricket club were experimenting with a new 'ball and stick' game and

they came up with hockey and drew up new rules.

In 1886, the Hockey Association was formed by seven London clubs. Later in Paris, the International Hockey Federation (FIH) was formed in 1924, and the International Federation of Women's Hockey followed in 1927. The first International competition took place in 1895, between Ireland and Wales (3-0). The International Rules Board was also founded in 1895 and men's hockey first appeared at the 1908 Olympic Games in London. The British Army introduced the sport to the rest of the British Empire especially in India and Pakistan. India played brilliantly on the field and had a winning streak from the years 1924 to 1956 till Pakistan broke their lead in 1960 and the gold was interchanged between these two teams for over a decade. The International Hockey Federation has continued to grow and now consists of 112 member associations, spread out over five continents.

Ice Hockey, Canada's favourite sport, was an inspiration from the game of Field Hockey and the Irish game of 'Hurling'. The modern version of Ice Hockey was invented by a Canadian named J. G. Creighton and the first game was played in Montreal in 1875. The rules were drafted at McGill University in Montreal in the year 1879. Ice Hockey spread to the US in the year 1893 and by the 1900s it was being played in the UK and parts of Europe. The idea of the game is similar to

Field Hockey except that the game is played on an ice rink and the players have to wear ice skates. There are two opposing teams with six players each. The aim is to hit the puck into the rival team's net which is guarded by a goalie. Ice Hockey became a part of the Winter Olympic Games in 1924 and remains just as popular as ever.

Basketball

"Slam Dunk", "Shoot", "Dribble" - these are all words that are cried out hoarsely by basketball fans from the stands during the NBA games! These fans are not the only people to know about basketball, it is in fact, one of the world's most loved sports. Surely, everyone's heard of Michael Jordon and 'Space Jam' right!

Basketball was founded on a rainy day in the gym of the International Young Men's Christian Association Training School (YMCA), today known as the Springfield College. The game was invented by James Naismith who was trying to keep his students busy on that particular rainy day. The game was first played with a soccer ball and a peach basket as the

hoop! The ball had to be retrieved by hand by poking out the ball from a hole made in the peach basket. Metal hoops, a net and a board were finally thought of in 1906 and the soccer ball was substituted by a Spalding ball. With the help of Luther Halsey Gulick, Naismith devised the first 13 Rules of Basketball.

The first professional league for basketball started in 1898 called the National Basketball League and then there were many smaller organisations. This period saw the birth of the Original Celtics, who are sometimes known as the "Fathers of modern Basketball". College Basketball was founded in Geneva College when they went head-to-head against New Brighton, YMCA and won 3-0. In 1946, the well known National Basketball Association (NBA) was founded after the Basketball Association of America (BAA) and the rival League the National Basketball League (NBL) merged. There have been many basketball associations since then like the Philippine Basketball Association, National Basketball League (Australia), Women's National Basketball Association and so on.

Basketball went international with FIBA (*Fédération Internationale de Basketball*) or The International Basketball Federation. It was formed in 1932 by eight nations which were Argentina, Czechoslovakia, Italy, Greece, Latvia, Portugal, Switzerland and Romania. FIBA saw the introduction of the US Dream

Team which consisted of seasoned players like the legendary Michael Jordon and Scottie Pippen of the Chicago Bulls, John Stockton and Karl Malone of the Utah Jazz, Magic Johnson of the Lakers, Larry of the Boston Celtics, Patrick Ewing of the New York Knicks, Chris Mullin of the Golden State Warriors, David Robinson of the San Antonio Spurs and Charles Barkley of the Philadelphia 76ers. Since then, FIBA holds international basketball tournaments and the latest one was in 2010 hosted by Turkey. The United States team emerged as the winners by beating Turkey in the Finals. The FIBA is only second in importance to the Olympic Basketball Tournament founded in 1936.

Baseball

 A 'bat and ball' sport, which is the national sport of the United States of America and the leading sport in Japan, Cuba and the Caribbean, is baseball. Remember the movie '3 Ninjas Kickback' where Rocky, Colt and Tum-Tum have an adventure in Japan and at the end of the movie Colt hits a smashing home run? The sport that the three ninja brothers are playing is baseball!

The history and origin of baseball is shrouded in mystery. No one really knows who invented the much loved game of baseball. It is believed that it evolved from earlier folk games which used a ball and a stick. Some say that baseball has English origins and came from the English game of *'Rounders'*, but the Americans disagree. There are similar conflicting stories because there are games like *'Lapta'* in Russia, *'Oina'* played in Romania and *'Schlagball'* in Germany, where the play is much like baseball. The word 'baseball' was first heard in the United States of America in the year, 1791. The man who invented the modern version of baseball, which is how it is known today, was Alexander Joy Cartwright, also known as the "Father of Baseball". Cartwright founded a team on September 23, 1845, known as the New York Knickerbocker Club, who were the first team to play according to the rules set down by Cartwright. The sport was played in New Jersey at the Elysian Fields, Hoboken between Cartwright's Knickerbockers and the New York Baseball Club.

There was later a convention called for discussing rules and other issues related to the sport and this was followed by the formation of the 'National Association of Baseball Players' and was the first organised baseball league of its kind. The American Civil War also helped spread the sport to the rest of the country and its end saw the emergence of many more leagues. In

1868, the annual convention of the baseball league was attended by delegates from 100 clubs. In North America, the current professional Major League Baseball (MLB) teams are divided into the National League (NL) and American League (AL).

Baseball is America's favourite 'national pastime'. The sport is played between two teams consisting of nine players each. It is played on a unique diamond-shaped field. The players use a rounded wooden or hollow aluminium bat and a ball made of cork and covered with a stitched leather coat. The players wear leather gloves or mitts and the batter should have a sturdy helmet worn to protect the head and ear and not to forget, the ever popular baseball cap!

The aim of the sport is to score runs by hitting the ball thrown by the pitcher and touching a number of bases which are placed at strategic locations around the diamond-shaped field. The players take turns at hitting the ball while the pitcher and his team try to strike out the batter. If a batter gets struck out three times, then he or she is out. The game is made up of nine innings, where one turn at batting for each team is taken as an inning. The team with the highest number of runs wins.

Did you know that George Herman Ruth, Jr., also known as the famous 'Babe' Ruth, who was the New

York Yankees' star player used to place a leaf beneath his cap and change it every two innings, just for luck!

Rugby

 Rugby football is an entirely different ball game. Though similar to Football and American Football, rugby has its own unique appeal. It is a rough and tough sport, steeped in tradition.

If you are a rugby player or fan, then you will know about the classic beginnings of the sport and about William Webb Ellis. If you don't, then we'll tell you. It was in 1823, during a game of football at the Rugby School in England that 16 year old William Webb Ellis picked up the ball, completely breaking the rules and ran with it towards the goal, clever huh! Some people say that it is not true and that rugby and football developed almost simultaneously and were inspired from ancient sports. Many such ball games did exist in the ancient times as well, where the player ran with the ball, but the invention of Rugby is credited by most to the Rugby School and William Webb Ellis. Even the coveted Rugby Cup is known as the 'William Webb Ellis Trophy'. The sport spread to other schools and soon many clubs popped up with their own set of rules. This made play between schools rather difficult and so a meeting was held on January 26, 1871 and was attended by the representatives of the different clubs. They put their heads together and came up with a standard set of rules for the sport of rugby. The Rugby Football Union was founded as a result and the first international match was played between England and Scotland on March 27, 1871, where Scotland won hands down.

The International Rugby Football Board was formed by Scotland, Ireland and Wales in the year 1886. However, England gave the thumbs down and declined the offer to join. They felt that they should have been given a greater representation. England finally did join the IRFB in 1890 and it was agreed upon that all matches would be played under the laws of the IRFB. The IRFB soon changed its name to become the International Rugby Board (IRB).

There was an interesting divide in the game when the Northern Rugby Football Union broke away from the established Rugby Football Union to conduct their own competition. This happened in Australia as well as in New Zealand in 1907. The reason for this split was that rugby was being played by both the upper class southern clubs and the working class northern clubs consisting of Lancashire and Yorkshire. However, the northern clubs were forbidden from earning even

a penny from the matches. Thus, the working class players found it impossible to devote time to the sport as they had to earn a living. It was then that the Lancashire and Yorkshire clubs broke away from the Rugby Football Union and founded the Northern Rugby League and codified their own set of rules.

Rugby is a continuous sport played between two teams, each consisting of the first eight players called the 'forwards' and a group called the 'backs'. The aim of the game is to score a point by carrying, passing and kicking the ball in the in-goal area. The team with the highest number of scores wins the game.

Did you know that there is also 'Underwater Rugby' and 'Wheelchair Rugby'?

Tennis

"The ball is in your court"

 A racket-ball sport, which has won hearts all over the world, is tennis. The game has given us many star players like Rafael Nadal, Billie-Jean King, Roger Federer and many more.

Tennis has evolved from its beginnings as a pastime for the nobles to an action-packed global sport of the 21st century. Tennis is said to have originated in the 12th century in France from a sport called 'Paume'. This sport was played in a court with a ball that was struck by hand. Soon, leather gloves came into existence. The sport advanced when instead of using hands, rackets were thought of to hit the ball and were called 'Jeu de Paume'. At the beginning of the game, the players would shout out "tenez" which meant 'play' and that is how Tennis got its name. In the year 1874, Major Walter Wingfield acquired the patent rights for the equipments and rules and invented a sport called 'Sphairistike', which in Greek meant 'playing ball'. The sport was very similar to the modern sport of tennis as we know it today. The sport soon spread to various parts of the world like Russia, India and China.

In London, the first championships were played in 1877 in the premises of the famous All England Club, Wimbledon. The sport was introduced to America when a young socialite called Mary Ewing Outerbridge from Bermuda met Major Wingfield in 1874 and a new tennis court was laid out at the Staten Island Cricket Club in New York. The first American National Tournament was played there and the singles was won by O. E. Woodhouse, who was an Englishman. The doubles match was won by a local team of two.

On May 21, 1881, the United States National Lawn Tennis Association was created to codify the rules and organise competitions. The Association is now known as the United States Tennis Association. The very first U.S. National Men's Singles Championship, now called the US Open, was first held in 1881 at Newport, Rhode Island. Also popular in France, the French Open was held in 1891. Together, along with the Australian Open, these four events are called the *Majors* or the *Grand Slams*. The standardised codified rules were announced in 1924 by the International Lawn Tennis Federation, which is now known as the International Tennis Federation. For an annual competition between men's national team, the winner would win the prestigious Davis Cup and the women's team would win the distinguished Fed Cup.

Tennis can be played as singles or doubles, where the player attempts to strike a hollow rubber ball over the net into the opponent's court. There are different tournaments played all over the world and are based on gender or age. Then there are the famous Grand Slams with the Australian Open, the French Open, the Wimbledon Open and the US Open. Tournaments are also organised for players with disabilities, such as 'Wheelchair Tennis and 'Deaf Tennis'. This is one game which will keep you on your toes!

Golf

For some, golf is more of an obsession rather than a sport! A club and ball sport, golf has given us star athletes like Tiger Woods, Bobby Jones and so on.

The origin of golf is a little murky. Historians trace it back to the Roman game of '*Paganica*' in which a bent stick was used to hit a stuffed ball. However, there is general agreement that the Scots were addicted to a version of today's modern day golf (even though James the II of Scotland banned football and golf so that his soldiers could pay more attention to archery and the country's defence tactics!). There were various sports resembling golf which were played in Holland, France, Belgium and not to forget Scotland. It was the Scottish Baron James VI who introduced the sport to England when he became the king in 1603. No one had heard of landscaped greens at those times. In fact, the sport was played on rough land with roughly hewn-out holes and flat terrain.

The rules of the sport, as we know it today, were codified internationally by the governing body which was the R&A (ruling authority) - a merger between The Royal and Ancient Golf Club of St. Andrews (1754)

and the United States Golf Association (USGA).

The sport of golf consists of competing players who use various types of clubs, which have different purposes and the knowledge of which should be with every golf player. The player then selects a club and attempts to hit the ball into a hole on the golf course with the minimum amount of strokes. The sport is played on a golf course, which has a teeing area set off by markers; this is where the golfer starts the game. The golfer must "play the ball as it lies" which means that wherever the ball stops, the golfer must pick up from there. So it's going to be a little difficult if it falls into the water! The 'Rules of Golf' define that the main aim is "playing a ball with a club from the teeing ground into the hole by a stroke or successive strokes in accordance with the Rules." It means that one must have the minimum number of swings or the lowest score for the most individual holes during a complete round.

Golfers use a whole set of equipment, which is carried around by their caddies. The most important are their golf clubs. Each club has a shaft with a grip on the top and a club head on the bottom. There are three kinds of clubs - 'Woods', 'Irons' and 'Putters'. The 'Woods' are used for long distance shots, the 'Putters' are used for gently rolling the ball into the cup and the 'Irons' are perhaps the most used for different kinds of shots. The golf balls have a three to four layer design and are made of synthetic materials. They have a dimpled surface and are mostly white in colour. A 'tee' is what the ball is placed on before being hit. It is made of wood or plastic and is used only for the starting shot called the 'Tee Shot' or 'Drive'.

Boxing

'The manly art of defence', boxing is a hand-to-hand combat sport, which is popular worldwide. A great way to stay fit and a reasonable excuse to fist fight!

Boxing is easily one of the earliest sports ever played. It started when someone lifted a fist against another in play. The ancient Greeks included boxing in the Olympic Games because they believed that it was a divine sport played by the Gods themselves. It was Homer's 'Iliad' that first revealed to us the existence of boxing in ancient Greece. Just like it is popular worldwide now, it used to be popular in parts of the ancient world as well. Archaeologists have found evidence of fist fights in a Mesopotamian tablet of stone dated to be 7000 years old, Sumerian relief carvings from 3000 B.C. and an ancient Egyptian relief from 2000 B.C. Both the Sumerian and Egyptian

reliefs show bare fist fighting, while the tablet from Mesopotamia depicts fist fighting for prize winning.

The earliest proof of gloves can be found in Minoan Crete on the boxing statues found on the Prama Mountains. These gloves were probably made of hard leather thongs worn to protect the arms and wrists. The Romans went a step further and created the *'Cestus'*, which had iron or brass studs added to the leather gloves. The Rajputs of ancient India also had dangerous gloves, where the boxers wore similar cestus like gloves, except these gloves had steel claws like those of a tiger. A favourite move with these gloves was a knockout blow, which was a downward sweep of the claws and gouging out the eyes of the opponent. These fights were called the "*nukki ka koosti*".

Boxing, also known as the 'sweet science', has evolved from bare knuckle challenges to big money fights of today. The craze of boxing diminished after the fall of Rome, but came back with a bang in the 18th century with boxing's first recognised champion - James Figg in 1719. He made the sport popular all over England by giving lessons in the use of sword, cudgels, broadswords and fists and also sparring exhibitions. Figg became the boxing champion of 1719 and when he died, he was succeeded by his pupil, George Taylor. Rules of boxing were first introduced in 1734 by John

Broughton, when in a fight against George Stevenson of Hull, he defeated him with a fatal punch beneath the heart and Stevenson collapsed. He later died in Broughton's arms. This episode affected John so much that he introduced rules which had to be followed during a bout of boxing so that untimely deaths don't happen. Many great boxing stars emerged after Broughton, some of whom are Daniel Mendoza, John Jackson, Tom Cribb and so on.

There are different styles of boxing and every style has got more than one star fighters who are renowned for their boxing prowess. There are the famous Muhammad Ali and Gene Tunney, who were the 'Classic Boxers' or 'Out-Fighters', who maintained a certain distance between themselves and their opponent. Then there are the 'Boxer Punchers' like Sugar Ray Robinson, who fight at close range with power and technique. A 'Brawler' or a 'Slugger' depends on absolute punching ability and throws vigorous punches at his opponent. Some of the famous names in this category are Max Baer, George Foreman and Sonny Liston. Another style is the 'Swarmer' or the 'In-Fighter', like that of the well known Mike Tyson, Harry Greb, Jack Dempsey, who stay close to their opponent and throw a combination of hooks and uppercuts. The last boxing style is known as the 'Counterpunch', which is employed by defensive fighters like Salvador Sánchez, Jerry Quarry and Ricardo Lopez.

Formula One

"Vroom....Vroom!"

 This is one sport where you can experience the thrill of speed. Formula One is definitely the most-watched and exhilarating motor sport.

Formula One or F1, the high speed racing sport has its origins in the pioneering road races held in France in the 1890s, the German races in the 1930s and the early post-war years of Italian races. The first proper motor race was the 1200 km race from Paris to Bordeaux and was won by Émile Levassor in 1895. The first Grand Prix was held at Le Mans where Ferenc Szisz won with his Renault at 63 mph, which was considered a very high speed back then. It was in 1914 that the Mercedes of Daimler-Benz took the French Grand Prix at Lyons and introduced signalling from the pits, which were shallow emplacements dug by the side of the track where the mechanics could work on the cars during pit stops.

Originally known as Formula A, F1 picked up greatly in the 1920s and the 1930s. After World War II, the Formula One motor races were super charged and the track distance was reduced from 500 km to

300 km. The FIA or the *Federation Internationale de l'Automobile* announced a World Championship race and on April 10, 1950, it was won by Giuseppe Farina in his Alfa Romeo. This World Championship was known as the first 'International Formula One' race. Farina's Argentinean teammate, Juan Manuel Fangio won his next five World Championship challenges and his record stayed for 45 years till the renowned Michael Schumacher took his sixth title in the year 2003. Since the first World Championship, there have been many such great drivers like Stirling Moss, Ayrton Senna, Nigel Manson, Damon Hill, Alberto Ascari, Lewis Hamilton, Alain Prost and many more. In the 21st century, Ferrari rules the roost but it was not always so. There were others like Alfa Romeo, Cooper, Maserati, Lotus, BRM, and Tyrell that have some excellent records.

Formula One, a single seater auto racing sport, has two annual Championships - one for the Constructors, who are the owners of that make of cars like Ferrari, Toyota and so on, and the other race is solely for the drivers. This is a massive televised event with a world audience of over 600 million! This is quite expected because of the high octane energy surrounding the event. The race cars go up to high speeds of 360 km/h or 220 mph with engines revving up at the astonishing 18000 rpm. The cars have to be perfectly tuned and in sync with the aerodynamics, suspension,

tyre control and the electronics, which the car is very dependent upon. Apart from the talent of the drivers, the mechanical superiority of the cars and the race circuits are also equally important. There have been many race circuits, but there are some which stand out. Nowadays, the circuits are built from scratch so that the location of the corners and the cuts are known, but in the olden days, grit hard public roads were used. However, those roads were dangerous and came close to taking the lives of some drivers. So new circuits were built and only the Monaco street remains of the old circuits. The most famous circuits are the Buenos Aires track, Albert Park in Australia, the A1-Ring in Austria, the Bahrain International Circuit, Spa-Francorchamps in Belgium, Interlagos in Brazil, Silverstone in Britain, Shanghai International Circuit, Magny-Cours in France, Suzuka in Japan and many more.

Keeping Busy!

Hobbies & Activities

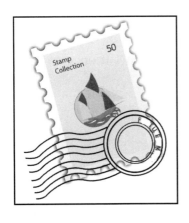

This section talks about a lot of hobbies to keep you busy! Hobbies which keep you fit and healthy, hobbies involving raw strength and mental ability and even hobbies where you can earn money! These and many more enterprising hobbies have been jotted down just for you.

Hobbies, which originally start as ways to pass the time, eventually go on to becoming life making careers. We hope that you will take to these hobbies similarly and make successful careers out of them!

In our list of interesting hobbies, we have activities which will keep you fit and help build up those muscles. They will also help in de-stressing your mind and bringing you peace from the tensions of life, like the drawing closer of the due date for your school assignment!

As you read ahead, you will find a variety of hobbies. Try out some of them and then pick your favourite pastime!

Paintball

Like all great games start from a small idea, so did paintball. This game definitely takes your breath away and knocks your socks off, literally! Paintball is an outdoor participation game played in almost forty countries. If you have a passion for adventure and the spirit of competitiveness, then this game is for you.

It was first thought of by Hayes Noel, who was a stock broker, Bob Gurnsey and author Charles Gaines, who wrote a photo essay called 'Pumping Iron' in the year 1976. Motivated by Gaines' hunting experiences in Africa and Richard Connell's short story 'The Most Dangerous Game', they decided to recreate the thrill of animal hunting and ended up inventing paintball. They created a scenario where they could stalk and hunt each other by using paintball guns.

This game is for all the adrenaline junkies out there. What better way to spend a day than by shooting paintballs out of a gun and seeing your opponent take a hit and actually fall rather than just playing pretend

war games in your backyard. Instead of playing war strategy games on your console where you are only pushing buttons and watching the action on the screen, you can actually be out there experiencing it for yourself in real-time. Paintball comes very close to the real thing. It's not just all about the fun, it also teaches you qualities like leadership, teamwork, strategic thinking and so on. In fact, big corporate company leaders indulge in these games so that they can build trust and strengthen their teamwork, which helps a lot in the boardroom and also acts as a great stress reliever. Not only corporates, but also the military have training sessions where they indulge in a similar character-building sport. It helps their speed, agility, intelligence, determination and their ability to think quickly in tough situations.

The equipment used in this sport is very interesting. The three main components of paintball are the paintball gun (also called a paintball marker), the paintballs (the ammunition!) and a pair of mask or goggles. There are many different kinds of paintball guns in the market, but they all do the same job of propelling the paintball to mark a rival team member. A loader is attached to the gun, which can be either gravity-fed or electronically-fed to ensure that the paint balls keep dropping into the chamber. Next is the paintball, which is a small round capsule full of colouring dye that is non-toxic and water-soluble and coated in a thin shell, which immediately breaks upon making contact. The last is the pair of protective goggles, which the players have to wear all the time on the field even when the game is not in play. These masks cover the eyes, ears, mouth and sometimes, also have throat guards.

The first game of paintball was played in New Hampshire in 1981, where the twelve people who participated, split into two teams and used Nelspot 007 pistols to fire paintballs and capture the flag, which was the aim of the game. This sport is a combination of the game of '*Tag*' and '*Hide and Seek*'. The main aim of the game is to capture the rival team's flag while protecting your own team's flag. Players take the offensive by trying to eliminate the other team's members by shooting a paintball at them from a paint gun and thus marking them or their equipment with paint, which is regarded as elimination of the player. The more players of the other team you eliminate, the more the chance of securing your own flag and capturing the rival team's flag. The game can last for minutes or a few hours, depending on the gameplay.

There are different kinds of paintball games. One is the 'Woodsball', where the game is played in the woods and can be either about capturing the opponent's flag or eliminating the entire rival team. Another kind

is the 'Scenario', where paintball is played based on different kinds of scenarios, like the World Wars. A third kind is the 'Speedball', where the playing field has huge inflated balloon-like bunkers for the players to hide behind. The game is challenging and takes place in different kinds of fields and difficult terrains. There are various kinds of game strategies and you may find yourself up against a very smart opponent. So winning requires not only speed and strength, but also a clear and sharp mind.

An extreme sport without the risk of injury, paintball is *the* game!

Say Cheese!

Do you have an eye for detail, for colour and for depth? Have you ever looked at a breathtaking scenery and wished to capture it in your mind? Have you looked at an inanimate object and thought, 'This would look amazing from another angle and with a different kind of light catching it'? Do you click pictures of friends and family and render it in an entirely different way? If you have, then turn your love for photography into a bona fide hobby, and like all hobbies, it could go on to becoming your dream career where you get paid for doing what you love doing!

The amount of information available on photography is overwhelming and if you are a beginner, you might start seeing stars if you read up on all the information there is. The best thing is to start by yourself with a basic camera and a simple, specific goal in mind. Photography is a hobby which is easy to take up and quite fun too, however, it is a slightly expensive hobby as you will need a professional camera. Everyone thinks that there is a trick or technique to photography, but it is really quite simple. All you need

is a passion for photography or just simply the wish to capture great pictures. A little knowledge and lots of practice will go a long way to make you an amazing photographer. There is nothing more enjoyable than capturing pictures of wonderful moments and sharing them with others.

If you want to get started immediately, here's what you will need:

- Dedication

- Eyes - The ability to see and observe details carefully

- A little financial help from your parents

For a person starting a hobby in photography, a good, self-focusing camera is a great start. Maybe for your next birthday, you can ask your dad to get you an automatic focus camera or a self-focusing Single Lens Reflex camera. Next, choose a subject; it could be nature, inanimate objects, people, scenery, animals and birds or absolutely anything that interests you. For lighting, you can experiment with the natural sunlight outside or use the artificial light inside your house. The more you practice, the more you learn about photography and the more you will be able to develop your own style.

If you want to share your experiences with someone else, you can join a discussion forum on the internet where other photography enthusiasts are willing to share tips, advice and their own experiences. You can learn a lot from them. You could also join a photography hobby club. Not only will it help you improve your technical skills, you will also meet people with similar interests who will help you grow in this field. Photography clubs usually conduct field trips and picnics, which could be ideal for networking as well as picking up good photography tips. You can also attend free lectures and seminars by professional photographers. As you continue to take pictures and become more involved in your hobby, you will also gain more knowledge along the way and learn about different cameras, lenses, UV filters and other such equipment, which you need for advanced photography.

Today, there are so many amazing digital cameras available which allow even a beginner to click pictures like a professional. So investing in one of these might be a good idea. Of course, you will first have to sell the idea to your parents. But once they see your love and passion for photography, they will support you and get you the equipment that you'll need. You have to ensure that all your equipment is kept safely. You can buy a good bag where you can safely stow your precious (not to mention expensive!) equipment.

 **A Boy's Guide**

If you want, you can develop the pictures yourself, though for this you'll need a darkroom and a few more tools, which your parents may not be willing to spend on. But don't worry! You can also get them developed at any local photo studio or shop. You can even use any photo editing software available online to edit and improve your photographs. After that, buy a good album and display your pictures with pride. People will be amazed at the beautiful images and fun moments you have captured with your photography skills. Eventually, you will find a style that fits you best. Go out and have fun shooting!

Boy Scouts

Everyone wants to belong to the Boy Scouts. To be a member of this Scouting organization is something many boys dream of. The Boy Scouts were founded by Robert Baden Powell as an organization in 1908. He got the idea from his experiences in South Africa and India when he was serving in the British Army. Powell wrote 'Scouting for Boys' published in 1908 and then later tested out his ideas in the first scout encampment at Brownsea Island Scout camp. A few months later, the Boy Scouts organization was founded.

The Scout programme instils in its young members a high degree of self-reliance, sportsmanship, integrity, community service, culture and good leadership qualities. Not only that, Boy Scouts learn about their society, culture and heritage. The Scout programme is not only about the learning, one also has fun doing it. There are outdoor activities involved, which aim at developing character, physical fitness and resourcefulness.

A Boy Scout is between the ages of 11 to 18. There is a junior and senior group and the Scouts are formed in groups of twenty called 'Troops'. They are under the guidance of a Scout Leader. They engage in a

structured programme of outdoor activities, spending time together in small groups and sharing experiences and rituals where they learn the cornerstones of the Scout method, Scout Promise and Scout Law. Activities such as camping, first aid, aquatics, sports, backpacking, woodcraft and hiking take place, which emphasise good citizenship and decision-making and help cultivate an appreciation for the outdoors. There are even special interests programmes where the Scouts engage in their own area of interest. As a result, there are many countries which have updated their Scouts programme and introduced special interests programmes such as Air Scouts, Sea Scouts, Scouting Bands, Rider Scouts and outdoor high adventure.

The Troop is the fundamental unit of the Scouts. The Troop engages in activities such as camping, backpacking and canoeing. Troops usually meet weekly, however, there are also occasional Camporees and Jamborees. Camporees take place when all the Scout units from the local area camp together for the weekend. The Jamborees are similar but on a much bigger scale. These are events of a national or international level held every four years, where thousands of Scouts camp together for one to two weeks. Scouts from all over take part in various activities and competitions like games, Scoutcraft competitions, fishing, aquatics, archery, woodcarving, rifle and shotgun shooting, sailing, patch trading, backpacking, canoeing, caving and white water rafting.

So, if you are all about the adventure, joining the Boy Scouts should definitely be on the cards. It teaches you not only life skills, but also how to be a better person and help others.

Collectorama!

Stamp Collection

 Collecting old and rare stamps is a popular hobby. Stamps are small adhesive paper cut-outs, which have some amazing artwork on them. The stamps chronicle major national events and movements. It is an intriguing hobby and helps us learn about the cultures of other countries and our own country better. Stamp collection is also called 'Philately' and is of two types - one is the collection of unused, rare mint stamps and the other is the collection of used stamps.

Would you like to take' up stamp collecting as a hobby? If you are interested, but still a beginner, then we will show you how to go about it with a few of our tips.

To begin with, you should have a theme for your stamp collection. You can start with gathering stamps from anywhere and everywhere, used or unused. Once you have a collection of many stamps, you can sort them out according to country, people, national events, animals and so on. Then place the stamps appropriately in your stamp collection album according to your chosen categories.

Now you have started your stamp collection hobby on a very successful note. To continue and expand your album, you can ask around in your neighbourhood and see if there is a stamp collection hobby club. You can also find these clubs online on social networking sites. If you find one, then you can discuss your collection with other stamp enthusiasts and even exchange one for another. You can also go to your nearest stamp dealer and buy a whole pack of stamps from him. This will give you a vast range of stamps to sort out and can result in many engaging and busy Sunday afternoons. The pack will contain a vast variety of stamps covering diverse topics and different designs. This will motivate you to collect more stamps.

If your budget doesn't allow you to buy whole packs of stamps, then tell your family, friends and relatives to be on the lookout for different stamps and to give you any stamp that they receive in the mail. This will add a sentimental value to your collection. Now that you are hooked, you can even ask for packs of stamps as gifts on special occasions, like birthdays!

You can also inquire at your local post office for any updates on stamps - new and old. The people at the

post office will help you learn more about stamps. The best part about stamp collecting is to display your stamp album to your family and friends and tell them the story behind every stamp. However, for stamp collecting you will need certain tools and equipment. Don't worry; they are inexpensive and simple tools and are readily available.

- The first is a stamp collection album or any standard 3-ring binder should do.

- A stamp hinge to place the stamps carefully.

- Stamp tongs for picking up the stamps. We don't use our bare hands as the sweat or acid from our fingers could ruin the stamp.

- Glassine envelopes, which are made of special paper to hold your stamps.

- A magnifying glass.

- A stamp catalogue, which is helpful in identifying the stamps. (This is an optional tool.)

Coin Collection

Did you know that coin collecting was also known as the 'Hobby of Kings'? It is generally believed to have begun in the 14th century, and the first coin collector

was the Italian scholar and poet, Petrarch. This craze soon took over the European kings and nobles. During the 19th and 20th century, it increased in popularity and anyone and everyone of any age and status was collecting coins.

Coin collecting, just like stamp collecting, offers a lot of information and every coin has its own story to tell. Each coin reflects a story from the past and talks about great leaders, kings and so on. You don't have to be a king to practice coin collecting, in fact, you don't even have to be rich to take up this interesting hobby. Just a little bit of your own pocket money should do! It's easy and fun to start collecting on your own. You can simply begin with the coins jingling in your pocket. All you need for this hobby is an interest in coins, a sharp eye and a box to store your coins.

You can start by rifling through your pocket change - at departmental stores, flea markets and so on. The coin doesn't need to be worth anything. Just pick up whatever catches your eye, put it into a small envelope when you are on the go and later, add it to your collection at home. Other than a box for keeping your coins, you can also buy a magnifying glass and a can or box for storing the coins.

There are three kinds of coin collectors and you can belong to any one of them. The first is the 'casual coin collector', who collects coins just for fun and without any profit motive. The next kinds of collectors are the 'curious coin collectors' who are more than just casually interested. They buy coins from coin dealers to expand their collection. The last kind are the 'advanced coin collectors', who have a genuine interest in the coins of the olden times and even collect medals of ancient Rome and Egypt. They are different from Numismatists, who actually study coins professionally. Now that you know the different types, you can belong to any group you wish to and maybe, evolve your casual interest into something more of a study.

If you want to know more about coin collecting, you can join a club or buy a coin reference book. By joining a club, you will gain more experience and learn more from your fellow members of the club. They can direct you to coin dealers and show you more about coin collecting. A reference book on coin collecting also works just as well. The book guides you in the understanding and valuation of different coins. So now that you have all the information you could possibly want on coin collection, it's time to get started!

Hiking

"Walk the walk"

 Hiking is a great way to stay fit and commune with nature. A pair of sturdy hiking boots, a canteen of water, some granola bars, a long stick and you are set to go! (Actually you might need a few more things, but more about that later.) It's also a great way to bond with your pals or your family.

Hiking, also called backpacking, bushwalking, tramping or trekking, is cross country walking, usually in places like the mountainside where you need some serious gripping strength and a good pair of hiking boots! Of course, there are the blisters, small injuries, rashes and mosquito bites to consider, but what is that compared to the glory of conquering the top of the trail!

Walking is one of the best and easiest forms of exercise. So why not make it fun and indulge in a little hiking trip? Hiking is walking only when you go for a walk in the wilderness and rely on your skills and abilities to stay in the wilds. If there are hills or mountains near where

you live, then all you need to do is pack a backpack and go into the wilds. However, if you live on the plains and the only mountains you see are towering concrete buildings, then you can plan a holiday to the mountains where there are proper hiking trails and paths. You can bring a buddy along or make it a family trip.

Some hikes are day hikes where the hike begins and ends on the same day. Some can stay the night and resume the trail the next morning. If you are planning a day hike, then your backpack will be much lighter than if you were staying the night and camping in the woods. You can make it a fun picnic trip if you are going for a day hike with your buddy and carry a lighter load. You can ask your mom to help you pack a picnic lunch with sandwiches along with some fruits, nuts, chocolates and crisps and carry a few small cartons of juice to wash it down. But remember to pick up all the packets and boxes after you are done and put it back in your pack and not leave any signs of litter. The other basic things that you must carry are some extra clothes, a first aid kit, a map and water. However, if you are going for an overnight trip with your family, you will have to pack a much bigger gear, which should have all the necessities like a camping tent, sleeping bags, more than one pair of clothes, water bottles, a box of matches, compass and maps, a first aid kit and lots of food. Oh and don't forget your toothbrush!

Here are a few hiking tips that you might find helpful:

- Do some ground work beforehand and figure out your hiking trail carefully. Carry a field guide and sufficient information about the trail. This is where a map and compass will come in handy.

- Start early in the morning, so that you start out fresh in the cool morning weather rather than hike under the sweltering afternoon sun.

- Carry an annoyingly loud whistle, which helps if you need rescuing and cannot call out for help.

- Carry enough water and extra food so that you don't starve or get too thirsty. Hiking uphill can make you really hungry and thirsty.

- Pack in some fruits like oranges and pears, which have high water content.

- A penknife is really important on a hiking trip and so are a first aid kit and a flashlight with extra batteries.

- Carry raincoats, sunscreen and sunglasses, just in case.

Rappelling and Rock Climbing

Another great hobby to pick up is Rappelling and Rock Climbing. This hobby is fun, exhilarating, keeps you fit and provides an awesome adrenaline rush. It is physically and mentally challenging, but which guy doesn't love a challenge! To do this, you have to learn the ropes and that means actually learning about the ropes, harness and safety procedures. As much as rappelling and rock climbing pack in a thrill, it is also very risky.

Rappelling is also called Abseiling, which is a German term and means 'to rope down'. It is when you descend a vertical surface, usually the side of a cliff, using a rope and a harness to provide friction, which helps in the descent. If you want to try it out, then don't let the excitement of doing it get to you and hop into the harness immediately. Instead, if you are a beginner, you should go through the proper process of being coached into it. Also, take a professional guide with you the first couple of times.

Rock climbing is similar to rappelling, except that you can also do rock climbing indoors. Indoor rock climbing is fun, safe and supervised, and you can rent the equipment from the indoor climbing gym that you go to. However, it is nothing like going out there and doing some real rock climbing with real rocks! Just like rappelling, it requires strength and control and the use of the muscles in your arms and legs to pull yourself up the rock face. It also involves the use of specialised equipment and harness for safety reasons. So if you take up rock climbing, you must learn how to use the equipment, because once you have mastered them, half your rock climbing is done!

Here is some basic information about the rappelling and rock climbing equipment:

- The first thing you need to have are the ropes usually made of continuous braided nylon fibres, because even if you didn't have any other equipment, you can at least climb down using the rope. You must learn how to make rappel rope knots which join the ropes. All your ropes should be thick and sturdy so that they don't cut with friction on the sharp rock edges.

- Belay devices, which look like a figure eight, have two metal hoops that are capable of stopping the rope or passing it through smoothly. Belaying is usually used when there is a partner below you during rappelling. It means to secure the person who is rappelling with one end of the rope tied to another.

- The harness is a very important part of the climbing gear. It can be fashioned out of the ropes or have a carabiner (rings of solid aluminium with a spring-loaded gate that allows them to be opened) attached to the ropes to make a secure and comfortable harness. The carabiners are used for both, rock climbing and rappelling. The harness can also be a sewn harness, which consists of a wide nylon belt for the waist and leg loops for the thighs.

- A helmet is a good idea for both rappelling and rock climbing. It protects the head from any rock debris, which could fall from above.

- The next piece of equipment is a pair of leather gloves that have a good grip. These are usually optional, but you can use them if you want to prevent rope burn, which happens if you rappel too fast.

- Last but not the least, don't forget a pair of good, sturdy hiking or climbing boots.

Vroom...

Mean Machines

The wind streaking through your hair and whistling past your ears, the road ahead long and wide, trees and bushes whipping past you in a blur, the adrenaline rushing through you, it's the greatest feeling ever!

There is nothing compared to the thrill of handling a powerful machine on wheels with an almighty engine roaring away under you. In this section of mean machines, we have for you some of the most beautiful, breathtaking, dynamic, hardcore steel and metal creations made by man, which are going to bowl you over.

This list of hypersonic and compelling cars and brawny and dangerously fast motorbikes, fuelled by breakneck speed, is sure to keep you riveted to the pages. The section is fully loaded with information about these various gorgeous vehicles. Read up the material given and impress your friends with firsthand knowledge about the fastest cars and motorbikes in the world today.

So rev up, turn on the NOS and read on!

Cars

Has it ever happened that you start staring into space and daydreaming about cars and having the ultimate fantasy of one day owning one of the world's fastest rides? This happens a lot, especially during a very long-winded history lesson or a boring math class! All of us dream about having a fast, very expensive car with maximum acceleration, a high rpm (revolutions per minute), high engine power with dual overhead cams, great mileage and top of the line designs.

Some of us have a list of things we want to buy when we are older and rich enough! For some it could be a sprawling mansion in the country, for some owning a football team, others would like to have a roomful of the latest and favourite video games and for a majority of us, we would like to own a garage full of the world's fastest cars. If you don't already have a list, you can start one now and refer to our section of mean machines to see which cars make up your list. So rev up full speed ahead towards the next section of cars!

1. 2010 Bugatti Veyron Super Sport

Top Speed - 267 mph
Acceleration - 0-60 mph in 2.4 sec

Rated as the world's fastest car, the Bugatti Veyron is the best example of automotive engineering. Manufactured in 2010, this car has a W16 engine and an astonishing power of 1200 bhp (horsepower), something which was unheard of in a production car. Equipped with four enlarged turbochargers and big intercoolers, the Bugatti Veyron SS has a seven- speed DSG semi-auto transmission and a double wishbone suspension in the front and rear. It boasts of a chassis made of carbon fibre monocoque and lateral acceleration of up to 1.4 G at 6400 rpm. With 1500 Nm of Torque at 3000 rpm, the Bugatti Veyron certainly deserves its place on the top.

2. SSC Ultimate Aero

Top Speed - 256.18 mph
Acceleration - 0-60 mph in 2.78 sec

Manufactured by the Shelby SuperCars, the SSC Ultimate Aero claims second place in the list of the

world's fastest cars. It has a twin-turbo V8 engine with 1183 bhp. The SSC Ultimate Aero has a six-speed sequential manual transmission and a tarmac tearing torque of 1094 lb-ft at 6600 rpm. The car is outfitted with unequal length upper and lower A-arms, coil-over springs and remote reservoir-adjustable Penske coil-over shocks with anti-roll bar suspension in the front and rear. The car has a unique personality, and its sleek leather interior is enough to turn heads.

3. Saleen S7 Twin-Turbo

Top Speed - 248 mph
Acceleration - 0-60 mph in 3.2 sec

The Saleen S7 Twin-Turbo was manufactured in 2006 by Saleen. This mechanically slick car has an all-aluminium V8 engine and a chassis consisting of lightweight steel and aluminium honeycomb composite reinforcing panels. It has 750 bhp and six-speed manual transmission. The Saleen is not only a good looking car with its luxurious seats and aluminium accents, but also has double wishbones with anti-roll bar suspension in the front and back. This car handles

amazingly with torque revving up to 700 lb-ft at 4800 rpm.

4. Koenigsegg CCX

Top Speed - 245 mph
Acceleration - 0-62 mph in 3.2 sec

 Designed by the Swedish car manufacturer Koenigsegg, the CCX makes it to the fourth place on the list of the world's fastest cars. The CCX stands for 'Competition Coupe X', where the X signifies the 10th anniversary of the test drive and completion of the first CC car in 1996. With a twin supercharged V8 engine, this car packs in a six-speed manual transmission with a twin-plate clutch. This sweet ride can torque up at 678 lb-ft at 5700 rpm and has a double wishbone suspension with inboard hydraulic shock absorbers and anti-roll bar.

5. McLaren F1

Top Speed - 240 mph
Acceleration - 0-60 mph in 3.2 sec

The McLaren F1 is still one of the fastest cars in the world, even though it was made in 1994. A timeless

car, it sports a 48 valve, 6.1litre BMW V12 engine with variable valve timing and capacity of 6064cc. With a horsepower of 627 bhp, it can torque up to 479 lb-ft at 4000 rpm. The F1 sports classy double wishbones in the front and rear with longitudinal wheel compliance, which resists loss of wheel control. This smooth engineering gives the car superb handling characteristics. For the McLaren F1, it's all about driving perfection.

6. Ferrari Enzo

Top Speed - 217 mph
Acceleration - 0-60 mph in 3.5 sec

This smooth ride will make you want to show off all the time! Manufactured by Ferrari, the Enzo has a V12 engine with a capacity of 5998cc. This ultimate car has a carbon fibre and aluminium honeycomb chassis, the characteristics of which can be changed using the sensors of the 'Sky Hook' adaptive dampers within the blink of an eye. It has a six-speed, semi-auto transmission and a suspension of double wishbones in

the front and rear with variable adaptive damping. It has a horsepower of 650 bhp and can torque at 484 lb-ft or 657 Nm at 5500 rpm.

7. Jaguar XJ220

Top Speed - 217 mph
Acceleration - 0-60 mph in 3.8 sec

 Made completely from aluminium, the XJ220 signifies the top speed that the Jaguar aimed for, which was 220 mph. Powered by a 24 valve V6 twin-turbo engine, it has a capacity of 3495cc and a horsepower of 542 bhp. This car boasts a smooth bonded aluminium chassis with aluminium body panels. The XJ220 has a five-speed manual four-wheel drive transmission and aluminium double wishbones in the front and rear for race car suspension. This aluminium roadster has a torque of 476 lb-ft or 645 Nm at 4500 rpm.

8. 2005 Pagani Zonda F

Top Speed - 215 mph
Acceleration - 0-60 mph in 3.5 sec

This fast car comes from a collection of the famed Italian manufacturer, Pagani and is named after

five time Formula One winner, Juan Manuel Fangio. The car is equipped with a Mercedes Benz 7.3 litre AMG V12 engine and a horsepower of 650 bhp. A two seat coup, it has a chassis made mainly of carbon fibre with ABS vented disc brakes and a rear wheel drive. Its front and rear suspension has aluminium alloy A-arms with pull-rod springs, adjustable dampers and anti-roll bar. Its transmission is a six-speed manual with twin-plate clutch and a torque going up at 780 lb-ft or 1057.54 Nm at 4000 rpm.

9. Lamborghini Murcielago LP640

Top Speed - 211 mph
Acceleration - 0-60 mph in 3.3 sec

This roadster is a high performance sports car outfitted with a 6.5 litre V12 engine. One of the fastest cars made by Lamborghini, it has a horsepower of 632 bhp. With sophisticated mechanical design and an upgraded chassis of high-strength tubular steel frame with carbon fibre components, this ride has a six-speed manual transmission. It sports a four-wheel

independent system, hydraulic shock absorbers and suspension with dual front and rear struts and anti-roll and anti-dive bar. It has a torque of 660 Nm at 6000 rpm.

10. Porsche Carrera GT

Top Speed - 205 mph
Acceleration - 0-60 mph in 3.9 sec

Manufactured by Porsche and developed in 1999, the Porsche Carrera GT sports a water-cooled 5.7 litre V10 engine. The Carrera GT has five colour schemes ranging from black, fayence yellow, GT silver, guards red, basalt black and seal grey. The car has a clutch made of high-tech ceramic metal and the engine is placed low in the chassis, which not only gives it a race car look, but also improves its aerodynamics and lowers its centre of gravity. The Carrera GT claims a horsepower of 605 bhp and a torque of 435 lb-ft at 5750 rpm with a six-speed manual transmission.

...And those were the fastest cars that exist in the world as of now. Technology keeps advancing and newer and better cars are being made. Sometime in the near future, these reigning cars will be dethroned and their place will be taken by even faster cars with a record-breaking top speed and amazing horsepower. Now we take a look at some famous car manufacturers who have given us many incredible cars.

Toyota

Founded in 1937 by Kiichiro Toyoda, this Japanese company is now a multinational and active car manufacturer. It was recorded that in 2008, about 9237780 cars rolled off the production line. It has manufactured the most selling and bestselling car which is the 'Corolla'. Toyota also owns other brands like Lexus and Scion. An amazing fact about Toyota is that they also manufacture robots!

General Motors

GM or General Motors is an American company and is ranked as the second largest automaker in the world as per records during 2008. It has produced over 5657225 cars. Established by William C. Durant in 1908, it is the oldest car manufacturer. The most famous brands of cars produced by GM are the Chevrolet and the Cadillac. GM not only manufactures cars, but it also produces trucks and owns other divisions

like Buick, GMC, Opel, Vauxhall and Holden.

Volkswagen

"Das Auto"
The name literally means 'car for people'. Volkswagen is a German company founded in 1937 by Ferdinand Porsche, Adolf Hitler and Bodo Lafferent. It has its headquarters in Wolfsburg, Germany and includes various car brands like Bugatti Automobiles, Audi, Bentley Motors, Automobili Lamborghini, SEAT, Skoda Auto and heavy goods manufacturer, Scania AB.

Ford

Ford is the second largest American manufacturer, which completed 3514496 passenger cars in 2005. Founded on June 16, 1903 by an American industrialist Henry Ford, the company is also popular for its vans. It was Henry Ford who invented the assembly line for automobile manufacturing. He revolutionised production and could turn out a complete chassis every 93 minutes, as opposed to the 728 minutes it took earlier. Since then, Ford has been running steady and producing top-of-the-line cars.

Honda

This Japanese company was founded by Soichiro Honda in 1948. According to records in 2005,

Honda was just behind Ford in production and manufactured 3324282 cars, making it the fifth largest car manufacturer. Honda produces cars as well as motorcycles. They are the largest manufacturer of motorbikes and have even invented a robot named ASIMO in 2000. Apart from that, Honda builds every kind of bike including mountain bikes and even race bikes.

PSA Peugeot Citroen

PSA Peugeot Citroen, previously known as Peugeot Société Anonyme, is a French manufacturer of automobiles and motorcycles. They are sold under the Peugeot and Citroen brand, founded in 1976. Peugeot Citroen is the sixth largest manufacturer of cars. The company sells both Peugeot and Citroen cars and even though they have different sales and marketing strategies, they both benefit from the common technology and development.

Hyundai

The Hyundai Motor Company is a South Korean company and was founded in 1967 by Chung Ju-Yung. In 1998, Hyundai bought Kia Motors, another South Korean company and together, they became Hyundai-Kia. This automobile manufacturer is number eight on the list of largest car manufacturers with 2777137 cars in 2008. It has an Indian subsidiary known

as Hyundai Motors India, which is the second largest car manufacturer in India.

Nissan

Nissan Motor Company is another Japanese company that was founded in 1933. Along with Toyota and Honda, it is amongst the top three car companies in Asia. It has three divisions - Infiniti, NISMO and Infiniti Performance Line. It was recorded that it produced 2697362 cars in 2005. In 1999, Nissan entered into an alliance with Renault SA, which is a French company.

Suzuki

Suzuki Motor Corporation was founded in 1909 as Suzuki Loom Works by Michio Suzuki. It is the ninth largest automobile manufacturing company and sold more than 2.6 million units in 2008. Suzuki produces motorcycles, compact automobiles, all-terrain vehicles and many small internal combustion engines. They have three subsidiaries - Pak Suzuki Motors, Maruti Suzuki and Magyar Suzuki.

Fiat

Fiat Automobile S.p.A. is an Italian automaker and was founded in 1899 in Turin, Italy by Giovanni Agnelli. It is tenth on this list of largest car manufacturers with 2524325 cars manufactured in 2008. The Fiat S.p.A, which is an acronym for Fabbrica Italiana Automobili Torino, has won 'The European Car of the Year' award for an amazing twelve years!

...And now we come to the powerful...

Bikes

Lean, mean, mighty machines! This list of fastest motorbikes is going to get your pulse racing. Riding motorbikes is all about the skill with which you handle it, manoeuvre it and speed it up. A bike can be your best buddy when you want to take a spin by yourself with the wind streaking past you, down a long wide road under the open sky. If you are passionate about bikes, then this list is made for you.

1. Dodge Tomahawk

Top Speed - 300 + mph
Acceleration - 0-60 mph in 2.5 sec

This mean machine deserves to be number one on the list. Even though the Dodge Tomahawk is not a street-legal bike, it is definitely the fastest

bike around. This prototype with its unusual design has a Viper V 10 cylinder engine with a capacity of 8277cc. The Tomahawk is a four-wheel motorcycle with independent suspensions. It has an amazing horsepower of 500 bhp at 5600 rpm and can torque up to 525 lb-ft at 4200 rpm. It has a two-speed manual transmission and is manufactured by Dodge.

2. MTT Turbine Superbike Y2K

Top Speed - 227 mph
Acceleration - 0-60 mph in 2.8 sec

This slick bike is the world's first turbine-powered, street-legal motorcycle, created by Ted McIntyre of Marine Turbine Technologies Inc. It was first owned by American television host, Jay Leno who said that, "It's like the hand of God pushing you in the back". The bike is powered by a Rolls-Royce Allison 250 gas turbine engine and has a two-speed automatic transmission. With its all-aluminium frame, this baby has a horsepower of 320 bhp at 52000 rpm and torque of 425 lb-ft at 2000 rpm. The Y2K was also featured in the Warner Brothers movie, 'Torque'.

3. MV Agusta F4 1000 R

Top Speed - 187 mph
Acceleration - 0-60 mph in 2.7 sec

Next in line is the MV Agusta F4 1000R, manufactured by MV Agusta. This superbike sports a 16 valve, DOHC inline, four-stroke, liquid-cooled engine and a multi-disc wet clutch, six-speed cassette gearbox manual transmission. The front suspension has an upside down telescopic hydraulic fork with pre-load adjustment and rebound damping and a single shock absorber in the rear suspension. The bike has a horsepower of 174 bhp and a torque of 81.9 lb-ft or 111.00 Nm at 10000 rpm.

4. Suzuki Hayabusa

Top Speed - 186 mph
Acceleration - 0-60 mph in 2.8 sec

The Suzuki Hayabusa GSX 1300R is manufactured by Suzuki. The Hayabusa is the Japanese translation of Peregrine Falcon, the fastest bird on the planet whose main prey is the blackbird. This super bike sports a 1340cc, four-stroke, four cylinder,

liquid-cooled, DOHC, 16 valve engine. It has an inverted telescopic, coil spring suspension in the front and a link type, oil-dampened suspension in the rear. It has a horsepower of 197 bhp with a six-speed, constant mesh transmission. The 'Busa' can torque up to 97.8 lb-ft or 132.6 Nm at 7600 rpm.

5. Kawasaki Ninja Zx-14

Top Speed - 186 mph
Acceleration - 0-60 mph in 2.5 sec

The Kawasaki Ninja ZX-14, manufactured by Kawasaki, is their most powerful bike right now. This beast has a monocoque chassis and wind-tunnel developed body. Sporting a 16 valve, liquid-cooled, DOHC engine with 1352cc capacity and a fuel system of DFI with Mikuni 44mm Mikuni Throttle Bodies, it has a six-speed chain manual transmission. The front suspension has a 43 mm inverted cartridge fork with front adjustable rebound damping, and an adjustable pre-load and a rear travel of 121.9 mm with a UNI-TRAK twin-sided swing arm and adjustable rebound damping in the rear suspension. It is powered by 190 bhp and a torque of 113.5 lb-ft or 154 Nm at 7500 rpm.

6. Yamaha YZF R1

Top Speed - 186 mph
Acceleration - 0-60 mph in 2.96 sec

The Yamaha YZF R1, manufactured by Yamaha, is the first motorbike to have a cross-plane crankshaft, which is a crankshaft design for V8 engines with a 90 degree angle between the cylinder banks. It has a 998cc, liquid-cooled, four-stroke, DOHC, 16 valve engine and a six-speed chain manual transmission. The front suspension carries adjustable pre-load and rebound damping with an inverted fork and a 119.4 mm travel. The rear suspension has shock absorbers and adjustable rebound damping with a twin-sided aluminium swing arm. The bike has a horsepower of 175 bhp and max torque of 115.5 Nm at 10000 rpm.

7. Ducati 1098s

Top Speed - 180 mph
Acceleration - 0-60 mph in 2.8 sec

The Ducati 1098s is the seventh bike on this list. Manufactured by Ducati, this bike has a

water-cooled, 90° V-twin, DOHC engine with 1099cc capacity. It has a six-speed chain transmission with Ohlins 43 mm fully adjustable fork and 120 mm wheel travel in the front suspension and a fully adjustable monoshock with top-out spring, aluminium swing arm and a 127 mm wheel travel in the rear. It has a power of 160 bhp at 9750 rpm and can torque it up at 90.4 lb-ft at 8000 rpm.

8. Kawasaki Ninja ZX-11/ZZ-R1100

Top Speed - 176 mph
Acceleration - 0-60 mph in 2.5 sec

The Kawasaki Ninja ZX-11 was marketed in North America as the ZX-11 Ninja and the ZZ R1100 in the rest of the world. The Ninja is powered by a four-stroke, four cylinder, DOHC engine with a 1052cc capacity. It has a six-speed constant mesh manual transmission with a wet, multi-disc clutch. The front suspension has a 43 mm Kayaba, a 120 mm front travel and adjustments for spring pre-load with rebound damping. The rear suspension has a Kawasaki UNI-TRAK and a 112 mm wheel travel. The bike has a 110 Nm or 81.0 lb-ft at 8500 rpm torque and a horsepower of 145 bhp.

9. Aprilia RSV 1000R Mille

Top Speed - 175 mph
Acceleration - 0-60 mph in 3 sec

This no-compromise bike is manufactured by Aprilia and has a V-twin, four-stroke engine with a capacity of 997.62cc. The bike has a six-speed chain drive transmission and front and rear suspensions, which have upside down fork in the front and a 120 mm travel while the rear has an aluminium plate, monoshock absorber. It has a power of 137.73 hp at 9500 rpm and can torque it up at 107 Nm or 78.9 lb-ft at 5500 rpm.

10. Honda CBR1100XX Blackbird

Top Speed - 174 mph
Acceleration - 0-60 mph in 3.1 sec

At one time, the Blackbird was the fastest production bike around. Even today, it is still riding among the top ten fastest bikes in the world. It has a liquid-cooled, 16-valve, DOHC inline, four cylinder engine with a capacity of 1137cc. The Blackbird has a close-ratio

six-speed transmission and a front suspension of 43 mm HMAS cartridge-type telescopic fork while the rear suspension has a Pro-Link with a gas-charged HMAS damper and a 109 mm axle travel in both, the front and the rear. The bike has a torque of 119 Nm at 7250 rpm and can power up 152 bhp at 9500 rpm.

* All specifications of the cars and the motorbikes mentioned in this book are indicative only. For exact specifications, please refer to the manufacturers' websites.

Having Fun!

Entertainment

This section has everything that's enjoyable and fun! Great music, engrossing books and the latest and popular must-see movies; we have it all in here just for you.

Do you love reading? Is your nose always found buried deep in a book? Then here are few more genres of books that you would definitely enjoy reading. We also bring you a collection of books ranging from the hot and happening reads of today to the glorious classics of the yesteryears.

If you are a music aficionado, then we are sure that the different genres and their list of songs given in this book will only increase your music knowledge!

Read on and you will find some interesting movies listed in this section, ranging from the good old classics to the adventure-packed new flicks!

Go ahead and enjoy!

Music, the Soul Food

Introduction to Music

Music is like the food for our soul and there is not a single person in this world who doesn't like music. Like listening to Heavy Metal? Or Rock and Rolla? You might even be a bluesy fan? There are many different genres of music with different artists who have made quite a name for themselves in their field of music. This is why we bring to you some fabulous musicians from popular genres and a list of some great foot-tapping songs. Sing on!

Rock 'n' Roll

This is the genre of music which "shook things up" in the 1950s and 1960s. The term rock 'n' roll was coined by Cleveland disc jockey, Alan Freed. He did this to try and end the segregation between African-American, European and American music. This is why rock 'n' roll carries a lot of influence of the rhythm and

blues music and also draws on the lyrical melodies of recent European immigrants and the country and western music of Texans. The introduction of American Bandstand made rock 'n' roll hugely popular with the teenagers. Electrically amplified guitars, harmonicas and drums - all say rock 'n' roll! Rock 'n' roll appealed to audiences across the world, and soon every young boy was strumming away on his air guitar!

Rock 'n' Roll

AC/DC, "*Back in Black*"

The Beatles, "*Hey Jude*"

The Beatles, "*She Loves You*"

The Bee Gees, "*Stayin' Alive*"

Elvis Presley, "*Jailhouse Rock*"

Chubby Checker, "*The Twist*"

Rolling Stones, "*(I Can't Get No) Satisfaction*"

Bob Dylan, "*Like a Rolling Stone*"

Led Zeppelin, "*Stairway to Heaven*"

Doors, "*Light My Fire*"

Metal

A major genre of rock that emerged was metal. With its origins from psychedelic rock and blues rock, heavy metal is characterised by powerful singers, loud bass and drums and distorted guitars loud enough to wake the dead! This sub-genre has given us many amazing bands, players and singers. Read on and you'll find some of the most celebrated musicians and their songs of this genre.

Metal

Iron Maiden, "*Hallowed Be Thy Name*"

Iron Maiden, "*The Trooper*"

Black Sabbath, "*Iron Man*"

Judas Priest, "*Victim of Changes*"

Judas Priest, "*The Ripper*"

Metallica, "*Master of Puppets*"

Metallica, "*Enter Sandman*"

Motorhead, "*Ace of Spades*"

Europe, "*The Final Countdown*"

Slayer, "*Black Magic*"

Pop

This genre of music has nothing to do with the rhyme "Pop! Goes the weasel"! In fact, this genre takes its name literally from the word 'popular'. It is a genre that anyone can enjoy and you don't need to have prior knowledge about it. This genre is influenced greatly by music like jazz, country, rock, soul, classical, gospel and even rap. Pop music has a mainstream style, catchy tunes and a commercial appeal that's enjoyed by everyone. After all, it has a 'popular' charm!

Pop

Michael Jackson, "*This is It*" (Title Track)

Michael Jackson, "*Billie Jean*"

Kesha, "*Tik Tok*"

John Mayer, "*No Such Thing*"

Lady Gaga, "*Poker Face*"

Lady Gaga, "*Bad Romance*"

Katy Perry, "*Firework*"

Katy Perry, "*Waking Up in Vegas*"

Black Eyed Peas, "*I Gotta Feeling*"

Flo Rida, "*Right Round*"

R and B

A combination of jazz, gospel and blues, R&B stands for rhythm and blues, though some people say it also stands for rhythm and bass. Contemporary R&B music evolved from the traditional rhythm and blues and has a distinctly different sound than its forerunners like Bo Diddley and Chuck Berry. This genre combines elements of pop, soul, funk and so on. Contemporary R&B was made popular by famous and celebrated artists like Stevie Wonder, Diana Ross, Michael Jackson, Janet Jackson, Whitney Houston, Boyz II Men and so on. Today, we know R&B as music by amazing singers like Alicia Keys, John Legend, Jill Scott, Jennifer Lopez, Ashanti, 50 Cent, Beyonce, Akon, Rihanna, Usher, Jay-Z, R. Kelly, Kanye West, Chris Brown, Trey Songz and many more.

R&B

Whitney Houston, "*I Will Always Love You*"

Mariah Carey, "*We Belong Together*"

Kanye West feat. Jamie Foxx, "*Gold Digger*"

Destiny's Child, "*Independent Woman Part I*"

Ashanti, "*Foolish*"

Beyonce feat. Jay-Z, "*Crazy in Love*"

Chris Brown, "*No BS*"

Usher, "*Burn*"

Leona Lewis, "*Bleeding Love*"

Alicia Keys, "*No One*"

Jazz

Jazz was the first indigenous genre of music in the US to affect music worldwide. It is difficult to define and jazz artists say that "jazz should remain undefined, jazz should be felt". It is said to be the musical language which contains the rhythms of human life. Jazz has enjoyed significant periods of popularity such as the 'jazz age' of the 1920's, the 'swing era' of the late 1930's and 'modern jazz' in the late 1950's. Jazz is said to have originated in New Orleans in the 1890s and then reached Memphis, St. Louis and Chicago. It has many roots including the tribal drums of the Afro-Americans, gospel, ragtime and blues.

Jazz

Louis Armstrong, "*What a Wonderful World*"

Louis Armstrong, "*West End Blues*"

Ella Fitzgerald & Louis Armstrong,

"*Dream a Little Dream of Me*"

Norah Jones, *"Come Away With Me"*
Nat 'King' Cole, *"Too Young"*
Nat 'King' Cole, *"For Sentimental Reasons"*
Miles Davis, *"So What"*
John Coltrane, *"My Favourite Things"*
Frank Sinatra, *"One For My Baby"*
Billie Holiday, *"Summertime"*

Country

Country music has nothing to do with cowboy hats and boots. This genre is a blend of traditional and popular musical forms found in the Southern United States and the Canadian Maritimes. Country music has produced two of the top selling solo artists of all time - Elvis Presley, who was earlier known as "the Hillbilly Cat" and was a regular on the radio programme *Louisiana Hayride,* and contemporary musician, Garth Brooks. Early country was heavily influenced by the Celtic and Gaelic roots of the people in those "hollers." With simple arrangements and beautiful harmonies, it has also been called Mountain Music. It is performed primarily acoustic, with typical instruments including banjos and fiddles, with guitars and even the autoharp adding to this Celtic-Appalachian rooted music.

Country

Keith Urban, *"I'm In"*

Carrie Underwood, *"Undo It"*

Carrie Underwood, *"Jesus, Take the Wheel"*

Garth Brooks, *"More Than a Memory"*

Garth Brooks, *"Good Ride Cowboy"*

Lady Antebellum, *"Need You Now"*

Brad Paisley & Allison Krause, *"Whiskey Lullaby"*

Johnny Cash, *"I Walk the Line"*

Willie Nelson, *"Blue Eyes Crying in the Rain"*

Alabama, *"Feels So Right"*

Blues

This genre is an art form which is an expression of loss, disappointment, suffering and triumph. The blues music has its roots in African folk music during the Slavery era of African-Americans. This was sung when the African-Americans were struggling with slavery. The blues has been adapted over the years and has given rise to singers like Ray Charles and groups like Led Zeppelin, whose many earlier hits were renditions of traditional blues songs. Blues music continues its metamorphosis, but the roots of the blues are real and very deep and they are not going to disappear. It transcends time and makes this genre unforgettable. W. C. Handy is accredited with being the "Father of the Blues", not because he was the first to play it, but because he was the first to score the music down and get it published. So if you are feeling a little 'blue', just listen to some legendary blues music.

Blues

W. C. Handy, *"Memphis Blues"*

Mamie Smith, *"Crazy Blues"*

Muddy Waters, *"Mannish Boy"*

Muddy Waters, *"Hoochie Coochie Man"*

Willie Dixon, *"Spoonful"*

Pine Top Smith, *"Pine Top Boogie"*

Elmore James, *"Dust My Broom"*

John Lee Hooker, *"Boogie Chillun"*

T-Bone Walker, *"Stormy Monday"*

Robert Johnson, *"Hellhound On My Trail"*

 **A Boy's Guide**

Here is a list of some legendary singers who cannot go by without a mention and a few more different genres of music:-

Rock 'n' roll (1950s)
Elvis Presley, Chuck Berry, Buddy Holly

Rock (1960s)
The Rolling Stones, The Who,
Creedence Clearwater Revival

Rock (1970s)
Led Zeppelin

Americana
Dave Alvin, Johnny Cash, John Hiatt

Emo
Dashboard Confessional

Country
Hank Williams Sr., Patsy Cline

Jazz
Duke Ellington, Count Basie, Louis Armstrong

Folk
Woody Guthrie, Pete Seeger

Reggae
Bob Marley, Toots & the Maytals

Soul
Sam Cooke, Aretha Franklin, Otis Redding

R&B
Ray Charles, Etta James

Celtic
The Chieftains

Rap
LL Cool J, Run DMC, Eminem

Hip-Hop
Black Eyed Peas, Tupac Shakur

Apart from the above genres, there are singers who encompass several genres like the great Beatles, Joni Mitchell, James Brown (R.I.P.) and Bob Dylan.

For Bookworms

"Anyone who says they have only one life to live must not know how to read a book."
- Author Unknown

"If there's a book you really want to read but it hasn't been written yet, then you must write it."
- Toni Morrison

"I find television to be very educating. Every time somebody turns on the set, I go in the other room and read a book."
- Groucho Marx

Books help us escape into another world. When you were younger, some of you wanted to be swashbuckling pirates, dashing heroes, go on an adventure to a far off land, solve thrilling mysteries or rescue the damsel in distress. But the minute you were shaken out of your dream world, the beautiful picture would vanish from your daydreams and you would find yourself getting scolded for dozing off in class! However, there is a way to return to your far off land, which your parents and even your teachers will encourage, and this is by reading books. It doesn't matter which kind of book you like, just take your pick and start reading!

Did you know that there are different genres for different books? Some of you could be fans of science fiction, fantasy, mysteries, non-fiction or even romances. But do you often get confused as to which book belongs to which genre? And if you liked a book of a particular genre, but couldn't figure out which genre it was, we are here to help you. Below, we have a list of the main genres. Read on!

Science Fiction

This one is a favourite with all the science buffs out there (never mind if they don't know any science!). The storylines in this genre usually have settings in alternative timelines, time travel, outer space, robots, the future and even nanotechnology. The main protagonists are often those who understand the science or technology that contradicts the known laws of nature and in the end help to make the world a better place.

This genre contains an exciting amalgamation of intellectual and physical adventures, events, plots,

characters and so on. Science fiction is considered to be a genre that explores the question "what if?" In case of science fiction, there are many imaginary elements which use scientific data as basis for stories and focus on stuff like future worlds, time travel, space travel and so on. This is a genre where writers are given free reign of their imagination and create worlds which we can only dream about.

Mysteries

We have all read the whodunits and the detective and spy thrillers that are always so engrossing and have us itching to read the last page to find out who the villain is. Books like 'The Adventures of Sherlock Holmes' or Agatha Christie's immaculate character, Hercule Poirot, have inspired all of us and at one time, even influenced us to become amateur detectives and solve the mystery of who stole our neighbour's cat! In this genre, there is a main protagonist, who gets involved in a mystery which has many characters and tries to discover a vital piece of information which is kept hidden until the climax. The main character investigates a crime or tries and solves various puzzles, just like the Hardy Boys. However, there can be more than one detective just like in our very favourite childhood books about the Famous Five or The Secret Seven!

Fantasy

When you were younger, you would have surely read Peter Pan, Wizard of Oz, Alice in Wonderland, Pinocchio, The Hobbit and many more. These are all great examples of the genre of fantasy. A fantasy book has events, places and people who seem make-believe and not realistic such as having magical powers, talking animals, sword fights, quests, dragons, witches and wizards. The best examples of fantasy are fairy tales, the kind we used to love reading and still do. With its roots in myth and legend, fantasy is the most elemental of all the genres. Another description of a fantasy novel is a book that contains unrealistic settings or magic, often set in a parallel universe or possibly involving mythical beings or supernatural forms as a primary element of the plot, theme or setting. Something magical is almost always a part of fantasy.

Horror

Have you read the bone-chilling Bram Stoker's Dracula, Shelley's Frankenstein or Stevenson's Dr. Jekyll and Mr. Hyde? These are all classic examples of the horror genre. Horror deals with the supernatural like ghosts, ghouls and unexplained phenomena. This genre evokes an atmosphere of fear and a sense

of emotional dread. One of the best-known contemporary horror writers is Stephen King. This genre is sure to scare, but if you are brave enough, you must read books of this genre!

Non-fiction

Non-fiction is the opposite of fiction. Non-fiction is a genre that is based on facts instead of on imaginary events. Writings from this genre involve a lot of research and also involves writing from personal experiences or narrating other people's experiences, events or even places. Non-fiction carries a little bit of fiction to spice things up. Examples of non-fiction include letters, essays, magazine articles, websites, speeches, autobiographies, biographies, memoirs, histories, reference books and diaries.

Romance

We know this is probably not high on the list of genres you would read, but it is one of the main genres of books and it won't hurt to know a little about it! The romance novel was originally developed in the Western culture. This genre focuses on the romantic love between two people, how they come together, how their relationship develops and how they overcome obstacles together. The drama and plot of the story is always related to the core theme of romantic love, though there can be subplots that do not directly relate to the main relationship. The best thing about romance novels is the "happy endings" and everyone lives happily ever after. But not always; some famous romances like that of the widely acclaimed Shakespeare's 'Romeo and Juliet' does not follow this rule and has a tragic end. This genre has evolved throughout history, starting from the much loved classics such as Jane Austen's 'Pride and Prejudice' and Emily Bronte's 'Wuthering Heights' to the modern "chick-lit" novels, which are so popular with girls the world over. In fact, we can say that Jane Austen was the granny of all chick-lit writers of today!

Here are some other genres:

Historical Fiction

Graphic Novels

Biography

Autobiography

Courtroom Drama

Detective/Spy

Family Drama

Literary

Poetry

Sports

Suspense

Thriller

War

Western

Self-Help

Health and Fitness

Here are a few books, contemporary as well as the famous classics, which we recommend:

The Harry Potter Series by *J. K. Rowling*

Harry Potter and the Philosopher's Stone

Harry Potter and the Chamber of Secrets

Harry Potter and the Prisoner of Azkaban

Harry Potter and the Goblet of Fire

Harry Potter and the Order of the Phoenix

Harry Potter and the Half-Blood Prince

Harry Potter and the Deathly Hallows

The Inheritance Cycle by *Christopher Paolini*

Eragon

Eldest

Brisingr

His Dark Materials by *Philip Pullman*

The Golden Compass

The Subtle Knife

The Amber Spyglass

Percy Jackson & the Olympians by *Rick Riordan*

The Lightning Thief

The Sea of Monsters

The Titan's Curse

The Battle of the Labyrinth

The Last Olympian

The Lord of the Rings Trilogy by *J. R. R. Tolkien*

The Lord of the Rings: The Fellowship of the Ring

The Lord of the Rings: The Two Towers

The Lord of the Rings: The Return of the King

Artemis Fowl (2001) by *Eoin Colfer*

Artemis Fowl: The Arctic Incident

Artemis Fowl: The Eternity Code

Artemis Fowl: The Opal Deception

Artemis Fowl: The Lost Colony

Artemis Fowl: The Time Paradox

Artemis Fowl: The Atlantis Complex

Bartimaeus Trilogy by *Jonathan Stroud*

The Amulet of Samarkand

The Golem's Eye

Ptolemy's Gate

Books by *Charles Dickens*

The Pickwick Papers

Oliver Twist

The Life and Adventures of Nicholas Nickleby

David Copperfield

Bleak House

Hard Times

A Tale of Two Cities

Great Expectations

 A Boy's Guide

The Hitchhiker's Guide to the Galaxy

by *Douglas Adams*

Robinson Crusoe by *Daniel Defoe*

King Solomon's Mines by *H. Rider Haggard*

The Hardy Boys books by *Franklin W. Dixon*

Treasure Island by *R. L. Stevenson*

The Hobbit by *J. R. R. Tolkien*

The Adventures of Huckleberry Finn by *Mark Twain*

The Adventures of Tom Sawyer by *Mark Twain*

Dragon Rider by *Cornelia Funke*

Peter Pan by *Sir James Barrie*

The Wonderful Wizard of Oz by *L. Frank Baum*

To Kill a Mockingbird by *Harper Lee*

Catcher in the Rye by *J. D. Salinger*

All Plays by *William Shakespeare*

Classics by *Jane Austen*

Movie Buffs

"...Bond. James Bond."
- Dr. No, 1962

"My mama always said, 'Life was like a box of chocolates. You never know what you're gonna get.'"
- Forrest Gump, 1994

"You talkin' to me? You talkin' to me? You talkin' to me? Well, who the hell else are you talkin' to? You talkin' to me? Well, I'm the only one here. Who the f*** do you think you're talkin' to?"
- Taxi Driver, 1976

"Sea turtles mate..."
**- Pirates of the Caribbean:
The Curse of the Black Pearl, 2003**

"With great power comes great responsibility."
"This is my gift, my curse. Who am I? I'm Spiderman."
- Spiderman

 There is nothing like watching a good movie couched up on the sofa with your friends, sharing a big bowl of buttery popcorn, chips, nachos and discussing the visual effects, the creative vision and the gorgeous actress! Movies are of many kinds. Some of them are educational, some inspirational, some are just pure fun and a delight to watch.

The most popular movie genres are:

Action and Adventure – A favourite among boys of all ages, this genre has everything to keep you riveted to the screen. It involves danger, adventure, risk-taking and hazmat situations! Car chases, spies, terrorist plots, the 'good' guys and the 'bad' guys, this genre has it all. Movies of this genre are characterised by a fast plotline, lots of action, adventures in the desert or jungle, hidden treasure, skirmishes, races, shooting, fights stunts and special effects.

Comedy – This one is sure to get a lot of laughs! This genre includes traditional comedies as well as romantic comedies. It usually has a happy ending and the plots are easy-going and often deal with love affairs or a gossip scandal. Comedies are one of the oldest movie genres beginning right from the black and white silent movies (remember Charlie Chaplin!). It has now gone on to become one of the most popular movie genres.

Drama – This genre concentrates on plot development. Drama is one of the largest genres and has a number of forms. It includes epics, fantasy, science fiction, period films and old westerns and so on. It portrays intense characters, real-life situations and realistic plotlines. Many of these movies are true depictions of real-life events or people. So if you are in the mood for something dramatic, this is the genre to go for.

Family – In this genre, there is always something for the entire family. A movie of this genre is something both, parents and kids, enjoy. These movies are made in such a way that they appeal to almost all age groups. Movies of this genre are huge profit makers and enjoyed by everyone. Want to ask your parents for an Xbox? Soften them up first by watching a movie together from this genre!

Horror – An eerily spooky genre, these movies will have you sitting on the edge of your seat or peering out from under your blanket. This genre hooks audiences with ghosts, spectres, demons, monsters and everything scary and creepy that you can think of.

We have here for you a list of the most amazing and popular teen movies, ranging from action flicks to musicals and a few classics. So go ahead and start watching!

Action (thriller, adventure, comedy)

The Good, the Bad and the Ugly

Robin Hood

Vertical Limit

Pearl Harbor

Poseidon

Indiana Jones and the Raiders of the Lost Ark

Indiana Jones and the Temple of Doom

Indiana Jones and the Last Crusade

Indiana Jones and the Kingdom of the Crystal Skull

Agent Cody Banks

Agent Cody Banks 2: Destination London

Superman: The Movie

Superman II

Superman III

Superman IV: The Quest for Peace

Batman (1966)

Batman (1989)

Batman Returns (1992)

Batman Forever (1995)

Batman and Robin (1997)

Batman Begins (2005)

The Dark Knight (2008)

Never Back Down

The Karate Kid (1984)

The Karate Kid (2010)

Hancock

A Knight's Tale

3 Ninjas

3 Ninjas Kick Back

3 Ninjas Knuckle Up

3 Ninjas: High Noon at Mega Mountain

Eight Below

Snow Dogs

Ironman

Ironman 2

Hulk

The Incredible Hulk

Prince of Persia: The Sands of Time

The Book of Eli

The Fast and the Furious

2 Fast 2 Furious

The Fast and the Furious: Tokyo Drift

Fast & Furious 4

Die Hard

Die Hard 2

Die Hard With a Vengeance

Live Free or Die Hard

Rocky

Rocky II

Rocky III

Rocky IV

Rocky V

Rocky Balboa

Spy Kids

Spy Kids 2: The Island of Lost Dreams

Spy Kids 3-D: Game Over

National Treasure

National Treasure: Book of Secrets

X-Men

X2

X-Men: The Last Stand

X-Men Origins: Wolverine

Ghost Rider

Fantastic Four

Fantastic Four: Rise of the Silver Surfer

Hellboy

Hellboy II: The Golden Army

Speed Racer

Fantasy

Dungeons and Dragons

Inkheart

Pirates of the Caribbean: The Curse of the Black Pearl

Pirates of the Caribbean: Dead Man's Chest

Pirates of the Caribbean: At World's End

Bridge to Terabithia

The Water Horse

Peter Pan

Hook

The Mummy

The Mummy Returns

The Mummy: Tomb of the Dragon Emperor

The Scorpion King

The Scorpion King 2: Rise of a Warrior

Night at the Museum

Night at the Museum: Battle of the Smithsonian

Harry Potter and the Sorcerer's Stone

Harry Potter and the Chamber of Secrets

Harry Potter and the Prisoner of Azkaban

Harry Potter and the Goblet of Fire

Harry Potter and the Order of the Phoenix

Harry Potter and the Half-Blood Prince

Harry Potter and the Deathly Hallows

The Lord of the Rings: The Fellowship of the Ring

The Lord of the Rings: The Two Towers

The Lord of the Rings: The Return of the King

The Chronicles of Narnia:
The Lion, the Witch and the Wardrobe

The Chronicles of Narnia: Prince Caspian

The Chronicles of Narnia:
The Voyage of the Dawn Treader

Science Fiction

Transformers (2007)

Transformers: Revenge of the Fallen

Avatar

Jurassic Park

The Lost World: Jurassic Park

Jurassic Park III

Godzilla

Star Wars Episode IV: A New Hope

Star Wars Episode V: The Empire Strikes Back

Star Wars Episode VI: Return of the Jedi

Star Wars Episode I: The Phantom Menace

Star Wars Episode II: Attack of the Clones

Star Wars Episode III: Revenge of the Sith

2012

War of the Worlds

The Day the Earth Stood Still

Deep Impact

Armageddon

The Day After Tomorrow

Independence Day

Volcano

Twister

Jumper

E.T. the Extra-Terrestrial

Back to the Future

Back to the Future Part II

Back to the Future Part III

The Matrix

The Matrix Reloaded

The Matrix Revolutions

Drama (crime, biography, family)

The Godfather

The Godfather Part II

The Godfather Part III

Cast Away

Finding Neverland

Oliver Twist

The Hurt Locker

Into the Wild

The Pursuit of Happyness

Mighty Joe Young

King Kong (2005)

The Legend of Bagger Vance

Animation

The Incredibles

Wall-E

Ratatouille

Up

Kung Fu Panda

Monster House

Open Season

Finding Nemo

The Lion King

The Lion King II: Simba's Pride

The Lion King III: Hakuna Matata

Toy Story

Toy Story 2

Toy Story 3

Ice Age

Ice Age: The Meltdown

Ice Age: Dawn of the Dinosaurs

Shrek

Shrek 2

Shrek the Third

Shrek Forever After

Madagascar

Madagascar: Escape 2 Africa

Comedy

Home Alone

Home Alone 2: Lost in New York

Home Alone 3

Home Alone 4: Taking Back The House

The Pacifier

Cheaper by the Dozen

Cheaper by the Dozen 2

Big Fat Liar

Three Men and a Baby

Three Men and a Little Lady

Bruce Almighty

Young Frankenstein

Groundhog Day

Lemony Snicket's A Series of Unfortunate Events

Sports

Rookie of the Year

The Sandlot

Mighty Ducks

Remember the Titans

Bend it like Beckham

We Are Marshall

Friday Night Lights

Goal! The Dream Begins

Goal! 2: Living the Dream

Goal! 3: Taking on the World

Dance/Musical

School of Rock

Step Up

Step Up 2: The Streets

Step Up 3D

High School Musical

High School Musical 2

High School Musical 3: Senior Year

Grease

Grease 2

Charlie & the Chocolate Factory

Historical (romance, epic)

The Last of the Mohicans

Troy

300

Australia

The Three Musketeers

Kingdom of Heaven

Spartacus (1960)

Gladiator (2000)

Documentary

Hoop Dreams

An Inconvenient Truth

Fahrenheit 9/11

Looking Fit

&

Muscling Up!

Health and Fitness

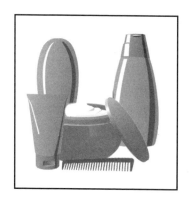

Health

Do you feel hungry most of the time nowadays and are always hanging on to the door of the fridge or pantry and moaning about how there is never enough to eat! Are you usually gorging on pizzas, burgers and all kinds of fatty foods and fizzy drinks, which contain absolutely nothing healthy? Well if you want to grow up to be a tall and fit guy, then you better start eating healthy now and load up on the nutrients, proteins and vitamins, no matter how yucky they sound!

It's essential that you eat food of high nutritional value rather than too many snacks that are rich in fat, sugar or salt. Try to eat some fruits, nuts and dried fruit as snacks rather than chips or sweets. After all, eating healthy is not only good for the body and mind, but it's also in vogue! People all over the world understand the importance of eating healthy and celebrities and sportspersons are also endorsing this concept.

Eating Healthy

A healthy balanced diet is rich in fruits, vegetables, starchy foods, with moderate amounts of meat and alternatives, milk and dairy products. Fortified breakfast cereals (and not the sweet sugary types!), margarine and fish, which is high in omega, are good sources of dietary vitamin that help ensure a good supply of calcium in the blood, which is essential for healthy bones.

Green vegetables are never a favourite; however, they are a must, along with brown rice and multigrain breads. Citrus fruits like oranges, lemons and tomatoes and vegetables like potatoes are all great sources of vitamin C. You can even make some refreshing juices, which go great with breakfast cereals and whole wheat toast!

Milk, margarine, butter, carrots and apricots are all good sources of vitamin A, which is great news because vitamin A gives you not only good vision, but also clear skin. So keeping away acne, which is something almost every teenager is afflicted with, becomes easier!

So guys, all you need to do to keep your body fit and healthy is to focus on eating a healthy diet and being active rather than stuffing yourself with easily available junk food. Exercising and participating in different sports will also help you remain fit and in shape.

Boys from the age of 12 to 15, going through puberty, experience a lot of hormonal changes. One of the most significant is a never ending appetite and a bottomless stomach! During the onset of puberty, boys have a sudden growth spurt, which leaves them feeling hungry most of the time and as a result, they indulge in fried and oily food. Teenage boys, who are active, require about 2800 calories a day and should eat foods containing minerals such as iron, calcium, zinc and magnesium, as well as vitamins. Calorie-rich, nutritious foods comprise of nuts, seeds and dried fruits or a bowl of muesli with semi-skimmed milk. If you are keen on building up your muscles, now is the time to do it with a good protein intake. So load up on the lean meats and poultry, fish, dairy products, nuts, pulses and eggs and steer clear of unhealthy trans fats and hydrogenated oils. You can always pack an extra ham sandwich that you can eat after a gruelling match and wash it down with milk or juice. If you are a veggie boy or don't eat a lot of meat, then substitute your meat products with plenty of fresh fruits, vegetables, nuts, seeds, dried fruits and pulses.

Eating healthy doesn't mean you can't go near pizzas, burgers, chips, aerated drinks or other junk foods. You may indulge in them once in a while, but just make sure they don't become your staple diet. You can also snack, in fact, snacking is good for you as long as the snacks are healthy. Eating between meals is something mothers frown upon, but if you choose healthy snacks like a bowl of breakfast cereal, a sandwich, toasts, beans, spaghetti, yoghurt, a yoghurt drink, a milkshake, a cereal bar, cheese and crackers, fruits, rice cakes, oat cakes and bread sticks, then even your mom will encourage it!

We have for you a table which charts the number of servings of different foods with their various nutrients.

Food Group	Fats, Oils and Sweets	Meat, Poultry, Dry Beans, Eggs and Nuts	Milk, Yoghurt and Cheese	Fruits	Vegetables	Bread, Cereal, Rice and Pasta
Servings	Use sparingly	2 - 3	2 - 3	2 - 4	3 - 5	6 - 11

Acne

Entering your teenage years is like the first stepping stone into adulthood. Every child looks forward to turning thirteen because they get to grow up just that little bit. It is, after all, the most fun years to be in. It's stress-free, with no responsibilities and you get to do anything you want... well, almost anything! But with the good always comes the bad. The one thing that we could do without during teenage, is acne. Teens get acne because of the hormonal changes that come with the onset of puberty. Acne is a condition that shows up as different types of bumps on the skin surface. These bumps can be blackheads, whiteheads, pimples or cysts. If your parents had acne as teens, then it is most likely that you will too. But don't worry; the good news is that acne clears up completely by the time you are out of your teens.

You may experience acne at some point during your teens, but don't fret. We have listed below some pointers which will help you keep your skin clean and acne-free.

There are too many acne prevention products available in the market these days, so how do you decide which one would suit your skin best and also prevent the acne from returning? You might end up buying and experimenting with various products and never find the right solution. But not to worry, here we give you some natural, homemade recipes, which are easy to procure and not really rocket science! You can make them yourself to help you fight acne and nourish your skin.

You can use almost any natural ingredient ranging from carrot juice, honey and cucumber. However, what works for one type of skin may not work for another. Make sure boys, that you don't mess up the kitchen during these little experiments!

Here are some natural remedies to choose from:

- To get rid of pimples, mix a little milk with nutmeg powder and apply it directly on the affected area

- Grind a few almonds along with egg whites (you can ask for your mom's help here) and add a few drops of tangy lemon juice. Make it into a fine paste and apply it on your face. Leave it on for about 15 minutes and then, wash it off with cool water.

- Another simple, yet effective, recipe is to mix equal parts of lemon juice with equal parts of rose water (you can ask your mom or sister for some rose water and say it is for a science experiment

at school!). Swish it around well and then apply it to your entire face. Wash it off with water when it dries. This remedy not only helps clear your skin, but also makes you feel refreshed.

- Last but not the least, beg a few pods of garlic from the kitchen and finely crush them. Add drops of clear honey and a small dollop of plain yoghurt. Mix it well and apply gently on only the affected areas. Wash it off carefully after some time, but don't scrub your face. Revel in the feeling of fresh and happy skin!

Here are a few other herbal options:

Tea Tree Oil

Tea tree oil, obtained from the *Melaleuca alternifolia* tree, is an essential oil that has a bacteria-fighting substance known as Terpenes. It is a light golden shade in colour and is a natural acne-fighting oil. You can also look for face washes which contain tea tree oil.

Olive Leaf Extract

Olive Leaf Extract is a very powerful, natural, herbal extract, the healing properties of which can be traced back to ancient Greece. It has extraordinary anti-bacterial, anti-viral and anti-fungal properties. Olive

Leaf Extract has therapeutic properties and is extremely safe to use as remedies for skin issues including acne breakouts. It can also be used to combat afflictions such as infections, fevers and coughs.

Licorice Root Extract

Licorice root, which grows freely throughout Asia and several European countries, is the most common and well known natural remedy for acne. It possesses anti-inflammatory properties and is able to clear up skin issues such as acne. It has long been utilised for medicinal purposes and consumption for thousands of years and is best for relieving upset stomachs and clearing up the skin.

Green Tea Extract

Green tea has long been used by the Chinese for medicinal purposes. Green tea helps reduce acne and inflammation. It is a hugely popular remedy and much less expensive than over-the-counter medications. Green tea is filled with antioxidants and has a natural astringent that soothes and heals the skin. The steeped green tea leaves act as a gentle exfoliant to help clear acne.

Aloe Vera

Aloe Vera extract is a gentle and natural cure for

pimples and acne. It has anti-inflammatory and anti-bacterial agents and is rich in enzymes. Aloe Vera helps in reducing blemish scars and also has immune-boosting properties. This extract will help keep the skin in good condition.

The best way to avoid acne is to eat healthy and eat right. Remember to drink lots of water, about 7 to 8 glasses a day! Maintain a balanced diet and a good intake of vitamin A foods like carrots, broccoli, milk and eggs. Wash and cleanse your skin thoroughly twice a day and make sure you get lots of exercise by running, jumping or indulging in your favourite sports!

Dandruff

It is one of the most annoying hair related problems. Let's first understand what dandruff is. It is not infectious or otherwise harmful, though it may cause social or self-esteem problems in some cases. It is a result of old skin cells renewing. When new skin cells grow, the old cells are pushed to the surface and look like white, flaky dandruff. The main cause of dandruff is the eating of wrong food, exposure to cold, harsh shampoos and general exhaustion. A well-balanced diet helps get rid of dandruff and also keeps it away. An anti-dandruff shampoo is also a very common treatment and it usually works well. If you want to go herbal, then there are few remedies that you can try out yourself. Here are some simple ways to get rid of those unwanted flaky, white bits.

- Hot oil therapy is the best remedy for dandruff treatment. Massage your scalp with liberal amounts of hot oil before going to bed. Next morning, say about an hour before taking your bath, rub lemon juice mixed in with cosmetic vinegar into your hair and then wash it off properly. For the last rinse, take the juice of one lemon in a bowl of hot water and wash it all off completely. Do this twice a week for about three months.

- A hot steam bath is great for removing dandruff and also for feeling relaxed. Massage hot oil (you can use almond oil for this) onto your scalp. Wrap a hot towel around your head for a few minutes and then go and wash it all off with your favourite shampoo.

- Fenugreek seeds are also an excellent cure for dandruff. Grind the seeds and soak them in water overnight. Massage the paste onto your hair, leave it on for about 15 minutes, and then wash it off thoroughly so that no trace of the paste remains. It may sound gross, but it's a great way to get rid of dandruff.

Body Mass Index

One of the biggest questions that girls and boys have as they grow and develop is whether they have the right weight. Don't worry - that's an easy question to answer. You can answer it yourself using the BMI. The right weight can be determined by the Body Mass Index or the BMI. The BMI is a calculation that estimates how much body fat a person has, based on his or her weight and height. The BMI is easy to calculate; all you have to do is divide your weight and height and then match it with the chart given across to see if you have the right body mass.

$$BMI = \frac{Mass\ (kg)}{[Height\ (m)]^2}$$

or

$$BMI = \frac{Mass\ (lb) \times 703}{[Height\ (in)]^2}$$

Category	BMI range – kg/m²	BMI Prime	Mass (weight) of a 1.8 meters (5 ft 11 in) person with this BMI
Severely Underweight	less than 16.5	less than 0.66	under 53.5 kilograms (8.42 st; 118 lb)
Underweight	from 16.5 to 18.4	from 0.66 to 0.73	between 53.5 and 60 kilograms (8.42 and 9.4 st; 118 and 130 lb)
Normal	from 18.5 to 24.9	from 0.74 to 0.99	between 60 and 81 kilograms (9.4 and 12.8 st; 130 and 180 lb)
Overweight	from 25 to 30	from 1.0 to 1.2	between 81 and 97 kilograms (12.8 and 15.3 st; 180 and 210 lb)
Obese Class I	from 30.1 to 34.9	from 1.21 to 1.4	between 97 and 113 kilograms (15.3 and 17.8 st; 210 and 250 lb)
Obese Class II	from 35 to 40	from 1.41 to 1.6	between 113 and 130 kilograms (17.8 and 20 st; 250 and 290 lb)
Obese Class III	over 40	over 1.6	over 130 kilograms (20 st; 290 lb)

Fitness

As you approach adolescence, you'll look for all the signs of your new maturity. Fuzzy hair on your upper lip, armpit hair, a croaky voice and that promised growth spurt which will definitely make you taller than the girls in your class! When it comes to puberty, for boys it's all about height and breaking the five-foot barrier.

Once you've hit puberty, you will have added muscle and height in your body and increased lung capacity. As a result, you will be a better athlete and have a higher self-esteem. Many teenage guys want to be like their favourite celebrities and sportsmen who they see on television and are ready and raring to go to the gym to get that bulked-up figure like the professional athletes. It's a great idea to participate in sports and exercise regularly, but guys, you need to be careful about overdoing it and straining yourselves. We have here for you some fitness tips that you will surely find handy.

Warming Up: The adrenalin running through you may make you want to jump into an intense workout, but it is very important to do some less intensive, warm up activities before you start your tough workout. Warming up loosens up your muscles and your joints and makes it easier to go through with your exercises. Also remember to stretch out once your workout is finished. This will prevent fractures and injuries.

Balanced Diet: A balanced diet is very important for you. As your body is developing, the right kind of food, along with healthy exercise, is really important for proper growth and development. It is also essential to intake a lot of calcium because at this stage your bones are more susceptible to fractures.

Enough Sleep: Getting enough sleep and taking proper rest is mandatory when you are a teenager. It is a great recuperation process that builds your strength and speed. You should be getting at least 8-10 hours of sleep every night, especially if you are working out. That means no midnight calls to your girlfriend and definitely no gaming late into the night!

Health Checkups: Working out should also mean frequent visits to your doctors or paediatricians every month to make sure you are healthy and well, to avoid any major injury or illness.

Resistance Training: All boys want to start doing

heavy weightlifting but if you are a teenage boy, it is advisable not to start heavy weightlifting until you are all grown up and have bypassed puberty. Instead, your focus should be on a resistance workout plan that emphasises low weights. It is also a great way to build bone mass.

The up side to exercising

Exercise happy bodies produce endorphins and make you feel great and peaceful. It helps you lose weight and lowers the risk of diseases. The right combination of exercises gives you increased energy and increased muscle strength. It decreases stress levels and helps you sleep well at night. Exercising enhances strength and stamina and also increases mental focus. This should help you concentrate in class and remember the algebra formulas! So exercising not only helps you physically, but also mentally, which will help you grade up in class. Exercising everyday gives you a great sense of accomplishment and boosts your self-esteem. We all know that a positive outlook and attitude goes a long way in life.

Keeping Fit

Walking

Walking is the easiest, cheapest and the most hassle-free form of cardiovascular exercise. Start slowly, then gradually increase your speed and distance. To keep yourself motivated and also to make it fun, you can bring along your best pal or girlfriend for the jaunt!

Jogging/Running

This is a step up from walking. Jogging puts a greater impact on the body as compared to walking. If you are starting an exercise programme, you must gradually move from brisk walking to running or jogging. If you have a dog, who is always ready for a run, you can take him out jogging with you. It will not only help you exercise, but also give your pet the run he needs!

Cycling

Riding a bike is not only fun and enjoyable, but it is also an excellent form of cardiovascular exercise. Always make sure to wear a helmet and follow the rules of the road. If you can master the cycle, then it won't be long before you can master the motor bike!

Swimming

A great way to beat the heat is to splash around in a swimming pool. Splashing, wading and paddling - means a great day in the water. Playing at the beach, at a water park, by a lake or in a pool can be a real treat on a hot day. The good news is that while you're having fun swimming, you are also giving your major muscles a workout.

Aerobics Exercise

Aerobics is a form of exercise, which increases the heat rate and gives a full-body workout. When you give your heart this kind of workout daily, it will become more efficient in supplying oxygen to all parts of your body.

Strength Training

You can do some strength training along with resistance training. Strong muscles help protect and support your joints during exercise. Building up your muscles will help you burn more calories and maintain a healthy weight.

Flexibility Training

Being flexible gives all the muscles a good workout. Flexibility training helps the body stay flexible and your muscles and joints stretch and bend easily. Doing yoga, martial arts, Pilates and gymnastics are a great way of building up flexibility. Being flexible also helps improve your sports performance.

If you are not much into working out, then you can always indulge in a sport. You can choose from team sports like football, basketball, cricket or you can go solo and pick out a sport like biking or skateboarding. As with all good things, it's possible to overdo exercise. Too much of a good thing is also not right. Exercising is definitely a great way to maintain a healthy weight, but too much of it isn't healthy. This is especially true for teens, who are still growing and their bodies need extra calories to grow properly. So, exercising too much can burn way too many calories than is necessary. Also, remember not to exercises when you are in pain or recovering from an injury as this will only worsen your condition. So go a bit easy on the exercise and gradually build up a workout programme, which you feel comfortable with and which doesn't stress you out too much.

So, there you have it, boys! Hope you found this book informative and enjoyable, because it was definitely a lot of fun to write. This book can be your constant companion during your teenage years and even when you are all grown up. You can share this book with all your friends and enjoy the various hobbies and entertaining activities together. Reading this book will give you the upper hand with other guys, when you show off and share all your knowledge about different hobbies, the happening music culture and some very fast wheels. So, like it was said in the beginning, this book should be read and re-read by you and get a priority position on your bookshelf beside your collection of favourite authors. Now that you have finished reading **A Boy's Guide**, *it's time to put all that you have read and learnt to full use and have fun doing it!*

A Girl's Guide

Sugar, spice and everything nice!

This book talks about everything in vogue - the best movies, latest bands and famous singers, the most celebrated music of different genres and some very enchanting stories to be read. It includes tried and tested tips on everything from delightful and engrossing hobbies, glam makeovers and a stylish dressing sense. Relationship advice and health tips are all included in this awesome book, which is the perfect gift for every girl!

ISBN: 978-81-7314-223-9 • Paperback • 180 pages • 129 X 198 mm